PURRFECT REVENGE

The Mysteries of Max 3

NIC SAINT

PUSS IN PRINT PUBLICATIONS

Purrfect Revenge

The Mysteries of Max 3

Edited by Chereese Graves

www.nicsaint.com

Give feedback on the book at:
info@nicsaint.com

facebook.com/nicsaintauthor
@nicsaintauthor

First Edition

Printed in the U.S.A

Prologue

Clarice casually licked her paws. She'd snapped up a few morsels and was taking a breather on the windowsill. Overhead, a full moon shone, and inside the house all was quiet. Just the way she liked it. Word in town had it there were rodents to be found at the beach house, and word hadn't lied. She'd snapped up a few critters and decided this place was a keeper. Usually she liked to hang out in the hills west of Hampton Cove, but since she owed allegiance to no one, being a free spirit and all, she went where she pleased.

Clarice was a feral cat, her hide a mottled reddish brown riddled with bald spots. Once, she'd belonged to someone. Some tourists passing through who'd gotten her for their kid. When she'd gotten sick in the back of their Toyota Camry they'd decided she was more trouble than she was worth, and had tied her to a tree and left her. Good thing some kind soul had come along and freed her, or she would still be fettered to that damn tree, chewing bark.

The beach house was a property that had recently gone through a major renovation. They'd taken a worn-out beachfront property, completely gutted it and turned it into a remarkable success story. Currently it was occupied by a sprawling family of exceedingly attractive females who'd come straight down here from Hollywood to film some scenes for a popular reality show. The three sisters lived in the main house while a small film crew had taken up lodgings in the guest house. The house was guarded twenty-four seven, but since no one ever stopped to frisk a cat, Clarice had easily slipped in and out.

Luckily for her the sisters didn't own a cat. Unfortunately what they did own was a nasty little yapper. A French Bulldog named Kane, who'd practically given her a heart attack when she'd entered the kitchen looking for some tasty little snack. The pooch wouldn't stop yapping. Sheesh. You'd think he had to pay for the food out of his own pocket. Good thing she knew how to handle a bully. She'd given him her best hiss and claw routine and he'd quickly run off with his tail between his legs, crying for his mommy.

She now sat licking her claws, savoring those final pieces of rat guts, when she noticed that something was going on inside the bedroom. She stared through the window and saw that someone had decided to play dress-up. They were donning a black gown that extended all the way to the feet and even covered the face, leaving only a tiny slit for the eyes.

The masked person was standing at the foot of the bed, staring down at the sleeping forms of one of the sisters and her husband. Way creepy.

She watched intently as the intruder brought out a rag and a small bottle and sloshed some liquid on the rag, then walked around the bed and pressed the rag against the face of the man, then reached over and repeated the procedure on the woman. This was no game. He or she was sedating them.

And then it got really freaky. Whoever was beneath that black robe suddenly reached inside the folds and brought out a shiny meat cleaver.

Clarice's eyes went wide with horror and shock when the robed intruder heaved the cleaver high and then let it drop down with a sickening thud on the woman's neck. Ouch! She cut her eyes to the French Bulldog lying at the foot of the bed. The stupid mongrel was stoically staring at the scene as if everything was hunky-dory. How weird was that? And as she watched, she felt a little sick to the stomach. She knew all humans were nuts and some were a little twisted, like the guy who'd tied her to that tree back in the day. But this was beyond sick. This was some evil *Game of Thrones* stuff right there. After a while, she had to look away, her stomach lurching. And since she was Hampton Cove's resident Feral Feline, that was saying something.

* * *

When Damien woke up it was as much from the rays of sun caressing his tan face as from the strong sense of nausea that assaulted him. It reminded him of that time he'd had plastic surgery, creating a cleft in his chin he'd hoped would add to his general look of cool dudiness. He'd woken up feeling just as nauseous from the anesthesia as he was feeling now. And then there was that smell. A pungent odor filling his nostrils and making him gag.

He groaned and rubbed his face. Did he have too much to drink last night? Nope. He and Shana had sat on the porch while her sisters cavorted in the pool. He hadn't felt like jumping in and neither had Shana. They'd had a huge fight, and neither had felt like having a romp in the pool or the Jacuzzi.

He cast a quick glance at his wife and saw she was fast asleep, judging from the bump under the sheets. Oh, Christ, he just hoped she wouldn't start screaming again. He hated when she did that. There was no real argument possible when she screamed her head off. The sense of annoyance suddenly returned when he thought about the predicament she'd placed them both in.

With a sigh, he swung his feet to the hardwood floor, fisting his toes.

Wow. He had to hold onto his head when a sense of vertigo assaulted him. It was as if the entire room was spinning out of control. He had no idea what was going on, but judging from that horrible taste in his mouth and that terrible smell, things definitely were not A-okay.

He stalked off to the en-suite bathroom and stuck his head under the tap, allowing the water to run over his close-cropped hair and into the marble sink. The cold water did him a world of good, and he almost felt human again. He toweled off his head and checked his face in the mirror. His skin was blotchy, eyes bloodshot. Nothing some makeup couldn't fix. Good thing the camera crew wasn't filming. He so didn't want to go on TV looking like this. People would think he'd had too much nose candy last night. Which he hadn't. With a marriage on the rocks he had no appetite for the stuff. If he got divorced, all of this would go away. No more Mr. Big Shot Fancy Pants.

He walked back into the room and was surprised Shana wasn't up yet. All his stomping around and putting his head under the tap should have roused her by now. He took a deep breath and decided to get this over with. The mornings after a big fight were always the worst. He didn't know what to say and neither did she. Better to address the elephant in the room right away.

He sat down on the bed and gently shook her shoulder. "Shana, we need to talk," he said. When she didn't stir, he gave her a slight nudge. "Shana? Come on, honey. Things can't go on like this. I need some answers. Stat."

With a frown he noticed a spot of crimson on her pillow and

he started. What the hell... He slowly slid down the sheet to take a closer look. And as he did, his eyes went wide and all the blood drained from his face. He would have screamed but no sound came. Later he didn't even remember staggering from the bed, falling to the floor and scrambling back, crab-style, to the door.

Like bile, a scream finally rose from his throat, coinciding with a scream that sounded from inside the house. He was up and racing down the corridor, and as he came hurtling into the dining room he saw Shayonne screaming her head off. When he turned to see what had set her off, he joined her in a long, protracted wail. Right there, in the middle of the table, was Shana's head, her eyes closed as if she were sleeping, her mouth open and biting down on a Jonagold, like a frickin' pig roast. A note was taped to her forehead, typed in Arabic script. And then he fainted and went down like a ton of bricks.

Chapter 1

Dooley, Harriet and I were seated next to the bed, staring up at our human, who was still fast asleep, even snoring a little. When Odelia Poole had taken me in, I'd vowed a sacred oath never to let her be late for work. And even though keeping my promise was a lot harder than I'd anticipated, on account of the fact that Odelia slept like the dead, I wasn't giving up.

I'd snuggled up to her, digging my claws into her arm while purring in her hair. I'd mewled, meowed and mewed up a storm. I'd even scratched the closet door, pounding it in a steady rhythm, and all I had to show for my efforts was Odelia muttering something unintelligible and turning over.

"She looks cute," Dooley said.

"Is she drooling?" Harriet asked.

"She always drools when she sleeps," I said.

"I think it's cute. She's almost like us," said Dooley.

"Not me," said Harriet. "I don't drool in my sleep."

"You snore, though," said Dooley. "It's so cute."

"Snoring isn't cute, and I don't snore."

"You do, too. Soft, little snuffles. Like a cute, little hamster."

"I'm not a hamster!"

"I didn't say you were a hamster. I said you sound like one. A cute one."

We went back to staring at Odelia. Her blond hair was a mess, her pixie face full of sleep marks, and her sheets were twisted and tangled as if she'd fought off Darth Vader in her sleep. And there was definitely drool. A lot of drool. As if she'd tried to scare off the Dark Lord by spitting at his helmet.

"All right," I said. "It's almost nine o'clock. She's going to be late."

The three of us were seated on the fuzzy pink bedside rug and could have sat there indefinitely, as the rug's softness felt great beneath my tush. But we had a responsibility. Being a cat isn't just about catching critters and looking cool doing it. It's about taking care of our humans while they're taking care of us. At least that's the way I see it. I may be an exception to the rule.

My name is Max, by the way, and I'm a blorange tabby. Yes, you read that right. I'm blorange. It's a color. It really is. A kind of strawberry blond.

"I think this calls for a serenade," Harriet said, licking her snowy white fur. She's a Persian, and pretty much the prettiest cat for miles around. She belongs to Odelia's mother, who lives next door, but she's in here all the time.

"A serenade?" asked Dooley. "What do you mean, a serenade?"

Dooley is a beige ragamuffin. You know, the kind that looks like a big, furry rabbit. Only he looks like a small, furry rabbit. A beige-and-white furry rabbit. Dooley is my best friend and neighbor. He comes with Odelia's grandma, who also lives next door. Yep. We're one big, happy family.

"I mean, a genuine serenade, like Romeo sang to Juliet?"

"Who's Romeo?" Dooley asked suspiciously. Dooley is secretly—or not-so-secretly—in love with Harriet, and jealous of every cat sniffing around.

Harriet rolled her eyes. "Romeo is a fictional character in a Shakespeare play. Don't you know anything, Dooley?"

Dooley raised his chin. "I know plenty. I know that Shakespeare is some dude who's in love, that's what I know. In love with Gwyneth Paltrow."

"That's not the real Shakespeare," Harriet huffed. "That's just a movie."

"Well, I don't see the point. There was no singing in the movie at all."

"I think Harriet is right," I said, deciding this was not the time for bickering. "We need to serenade Odelia. She loves our singing so much she'll wake up the moment she hears our sweet voices. Just like a radio clock."

"What's a radio clock?" asked Dooley.

"Oh, go away, Dooley," said Harriet. "Why don't we try the song we practiced last night? I'm sure she'll love it. She'll wake up gently and in a wonderful mood, completely refreshed. Like you said, just like a radio clock, but without those annoying radio jockeys jabbering about the weather."

"You mean *Sorry*?" I asked. "I don't think that's such a good idea."

"Why not? It was a big hit for Justin. I'm sure Odelia will love it."

"Who's Justin?"

"Oh, Dooley," Harriet sighed.

I stared at her. "Do you really think that song is appropriate?"

She laughed. "Appropriate? When is a love song *not* appropriate?"

"When is it?" asked Dooley, who had disliked the song as much as I had.

The thing is, Dooley and I had started cat choir a little while back, and had picked out a repertoire of cat-themed songs. You know, like *What's New Pussycat*. But when Harriet joined us she decided to glam up our repertoire, whatever that means. And then her boyfriend Brutus came along and took over conductor duties from Shanille, Father Reilly's tabby.

Things went downhill from there. Harriet started to dictate song choice, relying heavily on her mood. Last night she and Brutus had had a fight, and the big lug had us practicing Justin Bieber's *Sorry* all night. Oh, the horror.

We'd still managed, though, much to the chagrin of the neighbors, who hadn't liked our version as much as Harriet had. She'd been moved to tears when Brutus performed his solo and had responded by giving a rousing rendition of Celine Dion's *My Heart Will Go On*. It was all very disturbing.

"Oh, all right," I finally said. "Let's give it a try."

"Let's give what a try?" another voice now piped up behind us. I didn't even have to turn to know who the voice belonged to. Brutus happens to be my personal nemesis. The big black cat belongs to Chase Kingsley, who's the newest addition to the Hampton Cove police department, and has been making my life miserable ever since he arrived in town. He likes to think that just because his human is a cop he can lay down the law. And to add insult to injury, he's managed to snag Harriet's heart and dash all of Dooley's hopes.

"Oh, Brutus, sweetie," Harriet cooed. "We were about to try out that wonderful new song you taught us last night."

"That's a great idea, honey bunch," he said in that gruff voice of his.

He punched me on the shoulder, slapped Dooley on the back,

and we both toppled over. "Let's do this, fellas," he growled, and cleared his throat.

Brutus is just about the worst choice when it comes to conducting a choir. The cat doesn't have a single musical bone in his big-boned body. But that doesn't stop him from belting his heart out every time he opens his mouth.

I shook my head. At least when Brutus decided to tackle Justin Bieber, Odelia would finally wake up. Judging from the dozens of angry neighbors last night, and the half dozen shoes thrown at our heads, it was hard to sleep through the racket. Then again, waking up Odelia was what we were here for. She'd told me yesterday the Hampton Cove Gazette is going through a rough patch. Circulation is down, so she needs to buckle down and find a killer story. And the first rule to finding a killer story is getting out of bed.

"One, two, three," Brutus grunted. He'd taken position in front of us, his back to Odelia, like a genuine conductor. He was even swinging his paw just so, claws extended in case we hit a wrong note. Brutus believes in tough love.

"*Is it too late now to say sorry?*" Brutus bellowed at the top of his lungs. He was eyeing Harriet intently, who was giggling more than she was singing.

"*Cause I'm missing more than just your body*," she responded coyly.

"Oh, God," Dooley muttered.

"Hey! No bungling the lyrics!" Brutus yelled. "Be a Belieber!"

"I'm a Bebrutuser," Harriet tittered. "Is that all right, too?"

"It sure is, cutie pie," growled Brutus.

"Oh, God," I murmured.

"Hey!" Brutus repeated, and he slapped me on the head.

"Hey!" I yelled back. "No hitting the talent!"

"Who are you calling talent?" he said with a smirk.

"Oh, God," a tired voice came from behind Brutus.

He whirled around, ready to admonish her. But when he saw he wasn't talking to one of his choir flunkies, he snarled, "Look who's up!" instead.

"What was that racket?" she groaned.

"*Sorry*," said Harriet.

"That's okay. Just don't do it again."

"No, that's the name of the song."

"You could have fooled me," Odelia said, rubbing her eyes. "It sounded like a dozen cats being strangled, their heads chopped off with a lightsaber."

I know I should have felt offended, but I was so glad she was finally up I decided to forgive her. Not everyone appreciates great music the way us cats do, and the most important thing was that we'd finally achieved our purpose.

"Rise and shine, sleepyhead," I said. "Time to go to work."

"Ugh," was Odelia's response. "Just promise never to sing to me again."

"I promise," I said, crossing my claws. Until next time.

Chapter 2

I was glad we'd accomplished our mission, even though the awakening hadn't been as gentle and pleasant as I'd hoped. Odelia obviously wasn't a fan of cat choir, or Justin Bieber, or either. We probably needed to practice more. Then again, with Brutus at the helm we might never get to be as good as the Wiener Sängerknaben, my inspiration to start cat choir in the first place. Especially if Brutus kept hogging the spotlight to impress Harriet. It didn't impress the other choir members. And it didn't impress me.

We trudged down the stairs and padded into the kitchen, waiting for Odelia to join us, fresh from the shower and ready to start preparing breakfast. We didn't have to wait long. She breezed in, wearing ultra-short Daisy Dukes, pockets showing on the bottom, a canary yellow T-shirt that announced she was 'Crazy Cat Lady' and pink Converse sneakers. She started up the coffeemaker and switched on the TV to watch the news.

"Ugh. The Kenspeckles are still in town," she said as she dumped Corn Flakes into a bowl and poured milk on top of it and a few spoonfuls of sugar. “I keep hoping they’ll leave, but that obviously isn’t happening.”

“Who are the Kenspeckles?” asked Dooley.

We’d all hopped up on the kitchen counter barstools and were watching Odelia’s breakfast preparations intently. As soon as she’d finished preparing her own breakfast, we knew she’d start on ours.

“Just some family whose lives have been turned into a reality show,” she said. “The only reason I’m interested is because they decided to spend the summer in Hampton Cove and Dan keeps pushing me to do a piece on them. I’d rather poke my eye out with a fork than to come anywhere near them.”

“Why Hampton Cove?” I asked.

She shrugged. “Cause it’s the Hamptons. Cause it’s the place where all the cool people hang out. Cause after shooting a gazillion shows in LA they like to shake things up. I don’t know and I don’t care. I’m not a fan.”

That much was obvious. “You don’t like the Kenspeckles?” asked Harriet.

“Nope. Too much talk. I like a show with a little action and a great story.”

“Like *Game of Thrones*,” said Brutus, nodding.

“Yuck. A show where people’s heads get chopped off? No way.”

“I know what you like,” said Brutus. “You like to watch the game.”

She stared at him. “Game? What game?”

“Football, of course! At Casa Chase we watch it all the time.”

“At Casa Odelia we watch *The Voice*,” I said.

Brutus made a face. “*The Voice*? Are you crazy?”

“It’s all about singing, Brutus. I wouldn’t expect you to

understand."

"I like singing," he said with a quick glance at Harriet. "In fact, I love it. But *The Voice*? I thought you said you liked action and a great story, Odelia?"

"It doesn't get any better than Blake and Adam," she said, taking a seat and scooping up her flakes. "Add in some great songs and I'm hooked."

Brutus shook his head. It was obvious he didn't agree. "To each his own."

The sliding glass door in the living room opened and Odelia's mom walked in. "Good morning, family. And what a glorious morning it is."

A slim woman with long blond hair just like her daughter, Marge Poole was wearing hers in a messy bun this morning. Her white polka-dot shirt was belted with a thin leather sash and she was donning skinny black slacks. She gazed at us through horn-rimmed glasses and gave us a smile and a wave.

"Hey, Mom," said Odelia. "Aren't you the sight for sore eyes?"

"Oh, just my work clothes," said Mom with a deferential gesture.

Marge Poole was a librarian and ran the Hampton Cove library.

"I'd certainly borrow a book from you, Mrs. P," said Dooley.

"Dooley!" Harriet hissed.

"What? I would," said Dooley.

"She's a human and you're a feline. That's just wrong."

He frowned. "Why can't I borrow a book from her? I know my ABCs."

"Oh, you mean an actual book?"

"Of course. Why else would I go to the library?"

"I just thought..." She rolled her eyes. "Never mind."

"We were just talking about Chase," said Brutus.

"No, we weren't," said Odelia. "We were talking about the Kenspeckles."

"Chase is such a nice young man," Marge said. "And such a blessing for this town. Your uncle Alec keeps telling me he's so glad Chase decided to stay put instead of going back to New York to shoot with the big boys."

"Run with the big boys," Odelia corrected automatically.

"That's what I said. He could have had any job he wanted with the NYPD but he chose to stay in Hampton Cove. Isn't that just wonderful?"

"Super," Odelia murmured. "They should give him the keys to the city."

"I'm sure glad he stayed," said Harriet, practicing her best starry-eyed look on Brutus. "I don't know what I would do without my Brutus."

"Me neither, honey bunch," said Brutus.

Mom stood watching the syrupy scene with cocked head. "Aw, isn't that sweet? Young love."

"It's the best," muttered Odelia, not impressed.

"Shouldn't you be home with Chase right now?" I asked Brutus.

"Yeah, he'll wonder where you are," said Dooley.

"I'm sure he doesn't mind me spending the night with my girlfriend."

"I'm sure he doesn't," said Marge. "Chase strikes me as a man who appreciates love and affection. For a police officer he's very much in touch with his feelings." She gave Odelia a meaningful look.

Odelia threw up her hands. "Don't hold anything back, Mom."

"Well, I won't. Detective Kingsley is a wonderful young man, extremely handsome and very sweet and you could do a lot worse than him. And he's single, which I'm sure he won't be for long so you better move fast."

"I told you already. I'm not interested in Chase Kingsley."

"Someone else might snap him up. Alec tells me Blanche Captor comes into the office every day to file littering charges. She's in there at the crack of dawn, demanding Chase take her statement. And she just had that boob job."

"I'm sure it takes more than a pair of boobs to turn Chase's head, Mom."

"I'm not so sure. Chase might be a great guy but he's still a guy. And you know what that means." She directed a pointed glance at Odelia's more modest chest. "The women in our family have to rely on other assets, honey."

"Oh, for crying out loud, Mom," Odelia groaned.

To be honest, I've never understood this obsession with boobs. I mean, I'm a guy and I don't care one hoot about them. Then again, I'm not human, so maybe that's why. Truth of the matter is that Odelia has dated a few lemons in the past, so she's understandably cautious and I don't blame her.

"I think Chase is dreamy," said Harriet, contradicting her earlier statement that interspecies relationships are just plain wrong.

"And I think he's a great cop, but that doesn't mean he's relationship material," I said, deciding to put my two cents in. It seemed Odelia's dating life was a free-for-all now, so why not share my opinion with the group?

Mom laughed. "Oh, Max. Since when did you become an expert?"

I shrugged. "Just looking out for my human. Someone has to."

I like Marge, I really do, but I don't like how she tries to foist this cop on Odelia. To be honest, my motives weren't totally selfless. If Odelia hooked up with Chase, it wouldn't be long before he moved in and so would Brutus. If there was a way to prevent this doomsday scenario, I was all for it.

Marge patted me on the head. "You're doing a great job, Max."

"Thanks," I said dubiously. Compliments are a double-edged sword. You have to be careful or they blow up in your face. If it's swords that blow up in your face. It might be plans. I don't know. Hey, I'm a cat, not a dictionary.

"I think Odelia and Chase should hook up," said Harriet. "Just like Brutus and I have found each other. That way we'll all be family forever."

"I think you should listen to you cats, honey," said Mom. "They're a sacred and ancient species known far and wide for their infinite wisdom."

"I think Chase should return to wherever he came from," said Dooley, giving Brutus a particularly dirty look.

Odelia held up her hand. "All right, Mom. I'll listen to my wise cats."

"Dooley is confused, that's all. He is your grandmother's cat, after all. Some of her traits are bound to rub off on him and dilute his innate wisdom."

"I thought Gran wanted me to get together with Chase?"

"Gran wants to get together with Chase herself," said Marge with a tight-lipped smile. "Which is hardly appropriate for her age."

Odelia put her bowl in the sink. "You know what I think? This family is starting to resemble the Kenspeckles. If we're not careful we'll have our own reality show soon."

"Ooh, I'd like that," said Harriet. "I would love to be on TV."

"Oh dear God, no," said Marge. "Just imagine all those cameras filming everything we do. We wouldn't have a life anymore—no privacy at all!"

"It's all scripted," Odelia said. "Nothing about that show is real, Mom."

"Are you sure?"

"Of course I'm sure. Nobody behaves like that. It's completely fake."

"I think it's all real," said Harriet. "Especially the relationships. Nobody can fake all that love and affection. You can see it in their eyes."

Dooley and I rolled our own eyes. Odelia was right. Maybe *Keeping Up with the Pooles* would be the next big thing. Though *Keeping Up with Harriet and Brutus* would be an even bigger hit. Nobody could fake that much ignorance.

Chapter 3

The doorbell rang and Odelia was surprised to find Chase on the doorstep. She wanted to tell him they were just talking about him but thought better of it. Nothing boosts a man's ego as much as knowing a gaggle of women is talking behind his back, though she probably shouldn't include Harriet in this particular gaggle, as she wasn't an actual woman.

Chase Kingsley was tall, dark-haired and movie-star handsome and took his job very, very seriously. And whatever he was doing here probably had something to do with that job, because in all the time she'd known him he'd never once paid her a social visit unless she'd specifically invited him.

"What's up?" she asked, suddenly feeling a little underdressed. Those Daisy Dukes had seemed like a great idea half an hour ago, but now that Chase's eyes slowly traveled south and his eyebrows rose north, she was having second thoughts. Then again, there was nothing wrong with making a great impression, even if she wasn't interested in dating the guy.

"Morning, Miss Poole."

"Morning, Detective Kingsley. To what do I owe this pleasure?"

"There's been a murder."

"What? Who?" she asked, her smile evaporating.

"Shana Kenspeckle. They just found her."

Holy cow. "Give me a minute," she said.

He followed her inside, and nodded a greeting at her mother but ignored the cats seated at the kitchen counter. Unlike Odelia, Mom and Gran, Chase wasn't one of those rare humans who could communicate with felines. This special gift had traveled down from generation to generation because one of Odelia's ancestors had purportedly been a witch. It was a gift that came in handy in her line of work. As a reporter for the Hampton Cove Gazette she needed to be on top of everything that happened in her small Long Island town. And since she couldn't be everywhere all the time, Max and his friends acted as her eyes and ears, supplying her with a steady stream of news.

She drained her coffee cup and went in search of her smartphone.

"So what brings you down here, Chase?" asked Mom.

"Police business, I'm afraid, Mrs. Poole."

"Oh, for Pete's sake. When are you going to start calling me Marge?"

"There's been a murder, Marge."

Mom's hands flew to her face. "Oh, no!"

"Yeah. One of the Kenspeckle sisters was found murdered."

"But that's horrible!"

"I'm just going over there to investigate."

"And you're taking Odelia along? That's so nice of you, Chase."

He grimaced. "Chief Alec engaged your daughter as an official consultant to the department, ma'am, I mean Marge. He's made a point of including her in the day-to-day police business. And since he's out of town this week he's asked me to partner up with his niece for this particular investigation."

Judging from his tone he wasn't happy about Uncle Alec's decision.

"Oh, but that's wonderful," said Mom, clasping her fingers together as if in prayer. "The two of you together, cracking a case. That's so exciting!"

Odelia didn't know if it was exciting or not, but she thanked her lucky stars her uncle had made this arrangement. This way she could be where the action was, and didn't have to snoop around. Ever since he'd arrived in town, Chase had been reluctant to share information with her, considering her just another nosy reporter. Uncle Alec had quickly made it clear they did things differently down here in Hampton Cove, and since she was a great reporter he considered her an asset, not a hindrance. Chase had reluctantly complied.

"Let's go," he said a little gruffly.

"Let's go, you guys," she repeated to her cats.

He frowned. "You're not thinking about dragging your cats along?"

"Of course. They..." She searched for a good excuse. She couldn't tell him she wanted them to investigate. Talk to other cats. Figure out clues.

"They need the fresh air," Mom supplied helpfully.

"Then send them into the backyard," said Chase. "Plenty of air there."

"Sea air, Chase," Mom clarified. "It's good for their... complexion."

Chase had caught sight of his own cat and picked him up. "What do you think you're doing here, buddy? No wonder I couldn't find you this morning."

"Brutus and Harriet are an item now," Mom said with the sweetest of smiles. "You don't want to get in the way of true love, do you, Chase?"

Chase seemed on the verge of saying something scathing, but controlled himself. “Let’s just get going. I’d like to arrive before the coroner shows up.”

Five minutes later, they were riding in Chase’s squad car, which was a souped-up beat-up old pickup truck, four cats in the back and Chase looking a little glum. He clearly wasn’t happy about this new arrangement, and he wasn’t happy about having to drag four cats along for the ride either.

“So what happened?” she asked.

“When Damien LeWood woke up this morning he found his wife next to him. Only she was missing her head.”

“That’s not good.”

He nodded grimly. “It was found on the dining room table, an apple in her mouth and a note pasted to her forehead. The note was signed Al Kida.”

“Al-Qaeda?”

“Not exactly.”

He quickly showed her a picture on his smartphone. The uniforms who’d arrived on the scene must have taken it. The note was signed by Al Kida.

“That’s weird.”

“You said it.”

“Poor Shana.” She might not have been a fan of the show, but nobody deserved to die such a gruesome death.

He slid her a sideways glance. “So are you up for this?”

“Up for what?”

“Chief Alec wants us to handle this investigation together. I’m running point, as I’m the cop in this particular constellation, and you’re...” His lips tightened, as if he had trouble uttering the words. “... the consultant.”

"You mean like Richard Castle?"

"Who?"

"Rick Castle? From the TV show?"

He grimaced. "Something like that."

"So in this 'constellation' I'm Castle and you're Kate Beckett, right?"

He glanced over and she thought she detected a glint of amusement in his eyes. "Does that mean you'll get me one of those fancy espresso machines?"

She laughed. "Whatever floats your boat, Detective Kingsley."

He raised an eyebrow. "Whatever?"

A tingle languidly fluttered up her spine. Was he flirting now? No way. Chase Kingsley didn't flirt. "Within the boundaries of propriety, of course."

"I wouldn't have it any other way, Miss Poole."

Oh, boy. This was going to be interesting.

Chapter 4

They arrived at the beach house the Kenspeckles had rented for the summer. It was located along a strip of waterfront that was home to some of most expensive beachfront properties in Hampton Cove. This was where the other half lived. Each time she drove past the million-dollar McMansions she was impressed with the kind of lifestyle the rich and famous could afford. It was so far outside her own experience she felt like Alice in Wonderland.

The house the Kenspeckles had selected belonged to real estate mogul Merl Berkenstein. One of several top-tier properties the local estate agent had on offer. Merl had expensive tastes, which was probably why his offerings were so popular. When Chase's pickup slowed to a stop in front of the gate, she saw the black wrought-iron contraption was topped with gilded spikes and adorned with a lion's head captured in full roar. The Berkenstein logo.

Merl's business partner had a major stake in one of Hollywood's premier talent agencies, which was how he managed to entice so many A-listers to rent his properties. The ones that enjoyed staying here often ended up buying. They joined such luminaries as Steven Spielberg, Alec Baldwin and Jerry Seinfeld.

"Nice place," she said as the gate slowly swung open.

"Yeah, it's a great little pad."

"It's weirdly comforting that tragedy strikes even the best homes."

He glanced over. "Was that sarcasm, Poole?"

"I don't do sarcasm. Just an honest observation."

"I could have sworn that was sarcasm."

"Nope. Not sarcasm. Not me."

Chase sped along the caramel-colored gravel drive and she looked around at the perfectly manicured grounds. The lawn was as smooth as a baby's bottom, the shrubs sculptured to resemble Greek gods, and a smattering of angel and cherub statues dotted the landscape. Cherubs were a mainstay at Merl Berkenstein's properties. Maybe the man had a cherub fixation. Maybe his mother had given him a cherub pacifier and then taken it away.

The drive took a turn and the house loomed up before them. It was invisible from the road, which wasn't Merl's habit. He usually didn't like his houses to play peekaboo. He liked them to be visible from afar. To shock and awe with their sheer opulence and grandeur. To inspire envy. This one was designed to provide a measure of privacy, something she didn't associate with the Kenspeckles. When you make a business out of showing off every inch of skin and milking every emotional outburst to an eager audience it's hard to imagine there's anything left to hide from the public eye. Perhaps even the Kenspeckles drew the line somewhere, though it was hard to know where.

The house was one of those Jekyll & Hyde places: the front was completely different from the back. For some reason the architect had kept the facade intact but torn down the rest of the house. The front was classic Victorian. Large vaulted windows offered a look at the gardens, and a wraparound verandah with lime and pink columns prettied up the view. There was even a small tower with a gilded weather vane perched on top.

"Nice."

"Yeah, it's not bad," said Chase, parking his car in the circular driveway.

"Security is probably tight?"

"Pretty tight. The Kenspeckles brought along their personal security detail, then hired more muscle in town. They're not fooling around."

"And still they couldn't keep out the bad guys."

They exited the pickup and Odelia let the cats out. She gave Max a wink and watched the foursome traipse off. She had walked up to the front door before Chase stopped her with a wolf whistle. She turned to look and frowned at the circular sign he was making with his fingers. Obediently, she spun around. Chase laughed. "Not exactly what I meant, Poole. The front door is just that: a front. The actual entrance is around back."

Her cheeks reddened. "Why didn't you just say so?"

"I thought I did."

She jogged after him. "I figured you wanted to admire... the view."

He cut his eyes to her Daisy Dukes. "I'm not complaining."

She gave a silent groan. She knew she shouldn't have picked this outfit. She wasn't used to displaying so much skin. "Just thought I'd blend in."

A grin spread across Chase's features. "You stick out like a sore thumb, Poole. But in a good way."

What did that even mean? "Glad you approve."

At least she wasn't wearing a halter top. Her modest boobage was safely tucked away. Which was just as well. She wasn't wearing enough denim to cover her entire butt. Chase might get an eye twitch trying to take it all in.

Then again, he wasn't exactly a conservative dresser either. His tight buns were shrink-wrapped inside a pair of faded jeans and his muscular torso stretched a white cotton T-shirt to within an inch of its life. Classic but effective. If you've got it, you better show it. And Chase definitely got it. His dark hair curled down to his shoulders, accentuating chiseled features, a square jaw and chocolate eyes. The man was one mean man machine.

The only concession to whimsy was a cowlick that refused to stay put, dangling provocatively across his brow. Ever since she met the guy she'd been tempted to tame that cowlick. So far she'd been able to tamp down the urge. But if he kept checking out her butt like that, all bets were off.

They followed the gravel footpath that led round the house and she watched the structure morph from Victorian to twenty-first-century modernism. Unlike the facade, the rest of the house was all steel and glass. The second floor cantilevered over the first floor like a glass box, and the third floor jutted even further out, creating a futuristic effect. Pretty cool and just as outlandish as the family who now rented the place for the summer.

There was a flurry of police activity, and Chase moved inside with a sense of purpose that reminded her of Moses parting the Red Sea. She followed in his wake, glancing at the pool area that stretched out behind the house. The moment she stepped inside the dining room, the touristy fun stopped.

Right there, in the center of the dining room table, like some Roger Corman movie prop, sat the head of Shana Kenspeckle. The reality star's eyes were closed, an apple was stuck between her bleached teeth, and a note was glued to her forehead.

Odelia gasped at the sight. She'd seen Shana's face so many times, on TV and in the magazines, that to see it without its body was surreal. It was almost as if the woman had stuck her head through a hole in the table for some magic act. Any second now she could open her eyes, smile that enigmatic smile of hers and shout, 'Just kidding!'

But judging from the funereal atmosphere, and the grim-faced expressions of the uniformed officers stalking about, this wasn't a scene from some horror movie. This was reality. And then it struck her: whoever had killed Shana Kenspeckle hadn't just wanted to get her out of the way. They'd wanted to humiliate and debase her. Whoever the killer was had hated her.

Staring at the head was a short, paunchy man with hair like Doc Brown in *Back to the Future*. She recognized him as Abe Cornwall, the county coroner. In spite of his funky appearance he was a dedicated professional.

"So what have we got?" Chase asked.

"A dead body, a head and a weird note," Abe grumbled.

"Weird note?"

"One of the uniforms is Lebanese-American. She said it's the worst Arabic she's ever seen. As if the killer entered a few random lines into Google Translate and decided to call it a day."

"So it's not terrorists?"

"Unless Al Kida is a terrorist, I doubt it."

Chase stared at the note. "Gotcha."

Abe was right. Whoever had written this note had wanted to make it look like Al Qaida was behind the murder, but had managed to botch the claim.

"What about time of death?" asked Chase.

"Judging from lividity and body temperature I'd say she died between three and four last night."

"Body temperature?" Odelia asked. "Where's the body?"

"In the bedroom."

"Cause of death?" Chase asked, cool as a cucumber. As a

former NYPD detective he'd probably witnessed his share of gruesome crime scenes.

"My best guess is that she was drugged in her sleep, most likely with a chloroform-type substance, and then killed by decapitation with a meat cleaver or a similar tool. I'll have to check the lungs to be sure about the chloroform."

"She wasn't killed before they chopped off her head?" Chase asked.

Abe shook his head slowly. "Nope."

"Pretty gruesome," said Chase.

"Yep."

She followed the coroner and Chase down the corridor that led from the dining room to a suite of bedrooms. Like the rest of the house, the corridor was all-white: white hardwood floor, white stucco walls and white ceiling. Small prints of sailing boats were the only decoration. They passed several officers, who nodded a greeting, then shook their heads in warning. Uh-oh.

She walked into the bedroom. The body was still where the killer had left it, though someone had removed the bed sheets. The moment Odelia caught sight of Shana, she thought she was going to be sick. The woman's famous curves were clad in a red chiffon nightgown, and judging from her position she'd been fast asleep when the killer had struck. She was lying on her side, her double-D chest facing them, and if it wasn't for the fact that her head was missing, she could simply have been fast asleep.

"This is just too horrible," she muttered, her stomach acting up.

"Maybe you should step outside for a minute," Chase said.

He was right. She might be a hard-nosed reporter, but she suddenly felt as sick as when she'd had to dissect that frog in high school. She quickly walked out, leaving Chase and Abe to discuss the finer points of the murder. She'd get the details later. Right now she needed fresh air. Lots of fresh air.

She passed through the dining room, turning her head away from Shana's head, and stepped out onto the deck. Placing her hands on her knees, she took in big gulps of air, trying to convince her stomach to hold down her breakfast. It would be bad form to chuck up in the Kenspeckle pool.

She glanced up when two beige ankle boots appeared in her field of vision. They belonged to Shayonne Kenspeckle, one of Shana's older sisters.

"I'm... I'm so sorry for your loss," she said between swallows.

Shayonne nodded and darted a disapproving glance at her Crazy Cat Lady shirt and her Daisy Dukes. "Thank you. Who are you?"

"Odelia Poole. Special consultant to the Hampton Cove PD."

Shayonne gave her a cursory handshake, barely touching her skin. She was the spitting image of her sister, only with slightly coarser features, and instead of straight hair her dark hair was curly, with blonde highlights. She was dressed in a Dior top that announced she was the 'Sexiest Woman Alive,' a pair of cropped jeans, and designer sunglasses pushed up into her 'do.

"I was the one who found... the head," Shayonne said, closing her eyes and pressing long purple fingernails against her forehead, her lips trembling.

"I'm so sorry."

She opened her eyes. "Do you think they'll come for me next?"

"Who will?"

"Al Qaida. Isn't it obvious? We're being targeted by these terrorists."

"Oh, you mean the note. That was just a ruse, Mrs. Kenspeckle."

The woman stared at Odelia. "A ruse? What do you mean?"

"The killer tried to make it look like terrorists were involved, but they're not."

"They're not?"

"No. We'll have the note translated, but it looks like it's a fake."

Shayonne clasped a hand to her ample bosom and breathed a sigh of relief. "Thank God. I thought we were under attack. That I would be next."

"Well, you are under attack, but not from Mr. Albert Kida."

She wondered what the procedure was. Probably Chase wanted to interview Shayonne, but if she got a head start she was sure he wouldn't mind. They were a team. From the corner of her eye she saw Max and the others slink into view and disappear into the house. Which reminded her...

"Do you have any animals, Mrs. Kenspeckle? Dogs, cats... cockatoos?"

The last murder case she'd been involved in, the victim had owned a cockatoo, which had made Max's work very difficult. Cats and birds don't get along really well, and the bird had refused to divulge a single clue to him.

"Well, Shana has a French Bulldog," said Shayonne.

"Oh, that's right." She remembered now. Even though she'd told Max she wasn't a fan of the Kenspeckles, that didn't mean she hadn't caught a few episodes over the years. Perhaps even more than a few. "Kane, right?"

Shayonne nodded. Just then, the bulldog came waddling out. The moment he caught sight of Odelia, he started barking.

Arf, arf, arf.

"That's all right, Kane," said Shayonne. "Miss..."

"Poole. Odelia Poole."

Arf, arf, arf.

"Miss Poole is here to catch the bad person who killed Mommy."

Arf, arf, arf.

Shayonne swept Kane up in her arms and the dog stared at Odelia, his body trembling with hostility, a long slab of pink dangling from his mouth, his face puckered into a perpetual scowl. She didn't think Max would get a lot out of this Frenchie. Like cats and birds, cats and dogs don't get along.

"He's been barking up a storm all morning," said Shayonne, snuggling the bulldog and giving him a peck on his ugly little face. "You miss Mommy, don't you? Don't you, Kane? Mh?" And then she burst into tears. "Oh, God! She's really gone, isn't she? Gone for good! And to think the last words I said to Shana were that I hated her and that I wished she would just die!"

Odelia stared at the woman. "But... why?"

"Because she was sleeping with my husband, that's why!"

Chapter 5

We'd been sneaking all over the house but so far not a sign of a feline inhabitant. The only animal we'd met was some horrible dog who couldn't keep his trap shut. Just our luck: a murder had taken place and the only animal in the house was a stupid French Bulldog. I should have known going in that a family as peripatetic as the Kenspeckles would prefer canines to felines. And I was just about to give up when I caught sight of a rust-colored, scrawny cat, casually licking her paws while seated on a pool lounge chair.

Clarice, Hampton Cove's resident feral menace, looked right at home.

"Look, you guys," I said. "It's Clarice."

"Not again," Dooley cried, quickly covering his nose.

The last time we met Clarice, Dooley's nose had suffered because of the blood oath Clarice had made us swear in exchange of some information.

"Oh, no," said Brutus, for once agreeing with Dooley. "I'm not going anywhere near that monster."

"She's actually very nice once you get to know her," I told him.

That wasn't exactly true. Clarice wouldn't have looked out of place in a Quentin Tarantino movie. But for once I had Brutus at a disadvantage.

"Are you sure about this?" asked Harriet. "Last time Brutus got hurt."

"Last time Brutus fainted like a kitten," Dooley muttered.

"I didn't faint," Brutus countered vehemently. "I... I simply pretended to faint. I was trying to create a diversion so you could escape with your lives."

"Oh, that was so brave of you, Brutus," Harriet gushed.

"Looked to me like you fainted at the sight of blood," I said.

"Puh-lease," he scoffed. "Me? Fainting at the sight of blood? As if!"

"Look, Clarice is perfectly harmless," I said. "She's just... eccentric."

"Lady Gaga is eccentric, that cat is just... wacko," Dooley said.

"Wacko or not, we need her," I said, and stalked off in her direction.

I wasn't sure I was doing the right thing, but if we were going to find out who killed Shana, we could leave no stone unturned, even the wacko ones.

"Hey there, Clarice," I said as pleasantly as I could.

She gave me a cursory glance, but kept on licking her paw.

"What a great day, huh?" I said nervously. "Sun is shining, sky's blue..."

Still no response. I took a hesitant seat at the foot of the lounger. Clarice is a fount of information. She doesn't owe allegiance to anyone and roams Hampton Cove day and night, looking for food. She's familiar with every nook and cranny, and knows where all the bodies are buried since she's the one who buried them. Critter bodies, that is. She doesn't kill humans. I think.

"We, um, we're trying to figure out who killed Shana Kenspeckle," I continued. "You wouldn't happen to have seen something, would you?"

The others had joined us, but were keeping a safe distance. Dooley was still covering his nose, just to make sure Clarice didn't slice and dice it again. But Clarice simply ignored us, and kept on grooming herself. The pool was right next to the lounger, and the sun was reflected off the crystal clear water. It also reflected off Clarice's claw and I gulped when I saw she was watching me intently. I was suddenly reminded of Azrael, the Smurfs' mortal enemy.

I quickly looked away, and saw that the house was still a beehive of activity, with cops everywhere, doing whatever it was they were doing. Odelia was chatting with one of the Kenspeckle sisters, who was holding that nasty little mutt in her arms. For once the dog wasn't yapping furiously.

"That dog should be put down," Clarice suddenly said.

I was glad she finally spoke. I was even gladder it wasn't me she wanted to be put down. "I couldn't agree more. That dog is completely useless."

"He's been barking up a storm all morning, annoying the heck out of me."

"That's what he does. Yap, yap, yap. That dog has no off switch."

Great. We were bonding over our shared dislike of the canine species.

"That masked killer should have taken his head instead of the woman's."

I stared at her. "You saw the killer?"

Her eyes narrowed. "What's it to you?"

"I'm helping Odelia solve the murder."

She shook her flea-bitten, patchy head. "You don't get it, do you? When are you going to stop betraying your own species, Max? When are you going to get it through that thick skull of yours that humans are not your friends?"

"Odelia isn't like other humans. She takes care of us."

"Odelia loves us," said Dooley, overcoming his fear.

Clarice made a loud hissing sound, baring her teeth, and Dooley yelped and almost toppled into the pool. "Humans can't be trusted," she said. "They're mean and vicious. They chop each other's heads off!"

"You chop off the heads of mice and rats," Harriet countered.

"That's different. I would never hurt my own species." Her eyes narrowed into thin slits. "Though I might be tempted to make an exception for you."

Harriet gulped. Brutus, now that his mate was under attack, decided to step up. "Now look here, you... you cat. That is no way to talk to my girl."

"Girl!" Clarice emitted a series of low grunts that I figured was her way of laughing. "Cats don't have girlfriends! We don't mate for life!"

"Well, some of us do," Brutus said, winking at Harriet, who giggled.

"Well, then you happen to be an even bigger moron than I thought."

Brutus puffed out his chest. "Hey. Who are you calling a moron?!"

"You," she said. "You've lived with humans so long you've become one."

I had the sinking feeling this conversation was getting away from me. "Look, all we want is to solve this murder," I told her. "Is that so bad?"

"Yes, it is. By helping humans solve their murders you're perpetuating the species. As far as I'm concerned, the more they murder each other the better. Soon there won't be any humans left and this world will be ours again."

"Good luck with that," Dooley muttered.

I cleared my throat. "Be that as it may," I said, "I still would like to know who killed Shana Kenspeckle. It would mean a great deal to me personally."

"Why?"

"Um, because I'm a great fan of the Kenspeckles?"

"Of course you are. You're a disgrace to the feline species, Max. You and your friends. You have sold your soul for a can of cat food and a pat on the head. It's disgusting." She hopped from the sun lounger and stalked off.

"Wait!" I cried. "What about a big, juicy piece of raw meat?!"

She halted in her tracks and looked back. "What about it?"

"I, um, I've got one that has your name on it." No, I didn't.

She licked her lips and I could see she was torn between her reluctance to help us out and her desire for a nice piece of raw meat. "Tell me more."

I darted a pleading look at Brutus and he rolled his eyes. He knew just as well as me that I didn't have any meat to offer. "Chicken wings," he said reluctantly. "You can have one of my chicken wings."

"Go on."

He darted a dirty look at me. "And I'll throw in a couple chicken necks."

She stalked back to us. "Keep talking, fat boy."

Brutus growled something at the back of his throat. I gave him a poke.

"Chicken liver," he said. "Chase knows how much I like chicken liver."

"I'm starting to like you more and more, fatso. Don't stop."

He was shaking his head now, giving me a death stare.

"Just think how happy Chase will be when I solve this murder," I said.

"*You* solve this murder? *I* solve this murder," he growled. He cut his eyes to Clarice. "Raw, blood-red steak. Straight from the best butcher in town."

Clarice's upper lip curled up into a feral snarl. "You're now officially my new best friend. And where can I find all this good stuff?"

Brutus gave Clarice his address, which was actually Uncle Alec's address, since Chase was still living with him. It was taking him some time to find a place of his own in town. Not that he minded. Chief Alec was a widower, so the men had the house to themselves and were reliving their bachelor days.

"You never told us you ate steak," I told Brutus.

"Why would I share my steak with you, Max?" Brutus asked. "It's not exactly as if you rolled out the welcome mat when I arrived in town."

Now it was my turn to narrow my eyes. "That's because you've been trying to take over this town from day one."

He shrugged. "Just sharing my worldly wisdom with you local yokels."

"Brutus has offered me some of his meat," said Harriet. "It's delish."

"Of course it is," Dooley murmured, directing a pleading look at the sky.

"So do you want to know about this murder or not?" asked Clarice.

"Yes, we do," I said.

"I saw the murder," said Clarice. "I saw the whole thing."

"And?" Harriet asked excitedly. "Who did it?"

"No idea. The killer was covered in a long black robe."

"Like Severus Snape?" asked Dooley, who was a big Harry Potter fan.

Clarice blinked. "I have no idea who that is. All I know is that I couldn't see the killer's face, as he or she was wearing a black mask of some kind."

"Probably so they wouldn't get blood all over them," said Brutus. When we stared at him, he added, "What? Cutting off a head is a bloody business."

I didn't want to know how he knew. He, Uncle Alec and Chase probably watched too many horror movies. Or football games. They can get bloody.

"It was pretty gruesome," Clarice said, which surprised me. A lot.

"Oh, I can imagine," said Harriet commiseratingly. "Just tell us everything, Clarice. You'll feel so much better. It'll be like therapy."

Clarice gave Harriet her best glare, but the prospect of raw meat was still more enticing than the inconvenience of having to put up with Harriet. "The killer first held some kind of rag to Shana and her husband's faces, and then..." She closed her eyes, reliving the horror. "Then the sick bastard chopped off her head with a meat cleaver. I couldn't watch. The worst part? That stupid dog just lay there. Instead of defending his master, he simply took it all in. Just goes to show dogs are the stupidest creatures on the planet."

We all stared at Kane, who looked back at us, his tongue lolling. The moment he caught sight of five cats lounging by the pool, he blew a gasket. He jumped from Shayonne's arms and came running straight at us.

Arf, arf, arf.

"Run!" I yelled.

Arf, arf, arf.

I set off in the direction of the garden, hoping to find a tree high enough to escape this hairy monster. But instead of coming after me, he produced the sweetest sound in the world: the sound of a dog squealing in pain. When I looked back, I saw Kane racing toward the house, his tail between his legs.

"What happened?" I asked.

In response, Clarice showed me her paw. There was blood on her claws.

"Let's just say he won't bother us again," she said with a nasty grin.

Chapter 6

Odelia goggled at Shayonne. "Shana was sleeping with your husband?"

Shayonne nodded. She'd been momentarily distracted when Kane first jumped from her arms to chase Max and his friends, then raced into the house after getting his nose clawed by the ugliest cat Odelia had ever seen.

"Shana always had a craving for male attention. Even as a teen she tried to seduce every man she met. The fact that she was married to one of the greatest men alive apparently wasn't enough for her. She had to seduce my man, too. And Dion is weak, so weak he fell for her fatal charm."

"I'm so sorry," she said. "That must have been a great shock."

"It was," said Shayonne. She blinked. "Can we do this again?"

"Come again?"

"No, do this again. The big reveal. I feel I can do better."

Only now did Odelia notice the cameraman filming them.

"Um, what's going on?" she asked, a little perplexed.

Shayonne held up a finger while she closed her eyes. "Just a second. I wanna get this right." When she opened her eyes again, Odelia saw there were tears slowly rolling down her cheeks.

"Shana craved men," she said in a dramatic voice. "She was a natural born seductress who had to devour every male she met. The fact that she was married to one of the greatest singers of all time didn't stop her from hitting on my man. And Dion fell for it."

"Great take," said the cameraman, chewing gum. He was a chunky guy with a pasty face, patches of red hair peeping from under his Lakers cap.

"I still feel like I'm missing something," said Shayonne. "Oh, wait. I think I've got it." Once again, she pressed tears from her eyes, and said in a deep, sultry voice, "Dion is a weak, deeply flawed individual. And he fell for my sister."

"Love it," said the cameraman. "That's a keeper."

"Thanks," said Shayonne, wiping away her tears.

"How-how do you do that?" asked Odelia, fascinated.

"It's a trick," said Shayonne. "I think of dead puppies. Works every time."

"Dead puppies. Huh. Interesting."

"Yoo-hoo! Alejandro! Over here!"

She watched as a curly-haired man with olive skin walked up. He was the spitting image of Antonio Banderas, and oozed charm and male charisma.

"This is the director of the show," Shayonne said. "Alejandro Salanova." Odelia expected Shayonne to introduce her, but apparently she wasn't important enough. "Have you filmed the body?" she asked, sounding more like a producer than a mourning sister.

"Not yet," said Alejandro. "The cops won't let us. They say it's a crime scene and we're not allowed inside until they remove the body."

"Crap," said Shayonne, then turned to Odelia. "You're a cop, right? Can't you arrange for Alejandro and his crew to shoot the body and the head?"

"I, um..." Odelia was lost for words. She'd known the Kenspeckles had a show to run, but she'd figured this tragedy would put a stop to all of that. "Aren't you going to cancel the show now that your sister... is dead?"

Shayonne's eyebrows rose fractionally. "Cancel the show? Honey, this is the best thing that could have happened to us."

"We'll shoot right up in the ratings," said Alejandro. He stuck up his index finger for emphasis. "Numero uno, baby!"

"We've been dropping in the ratings," Shayonne explained. "It's time to reclaim the top spot again, and this whole murder thing just might do it."

She stared at the woman, wondering if she was a human or a robot.

Shayonne turned away. "Just muscle your way in there. Don't take no for an answer. Get a few good shots of the body and the head before it's too late."

And with these words she stalked off to give further instructions to Alejandro and his crew. Odelia watched them walk into the house and realized her jaw was still on the floor. She hitched it up and walked over to the loungers to join Max and the cats. She plunked down, shaking her head.

"The killer was wearing some kind of long black robe," said Max.

"Uh-huh," she said, watching as the cameraman started filming inside the dining room, ignoring the protestations of several police officers nearby.

"Clarice saw the whole thing. She was right there when it happened."

This time Max caught her attention. "She witnessed the murder?"

"Yep. She told us the whole story in exchange for a juicy steak.

Why does Brutus get to eat steak and we don't, Odelia? I like steak. We all do."

"Meat is expensive, buddy. A reporter's salary will only get you so far."

He shook his head. "Of course. I knew that. I'm sorry. It's just that..." He waved a paw. "That Brutus is driving me crazy. With his chicken wings and his chicken necks and his... his chicken liver."

"Just like his master," Odelia said. She watched as Chase and Alejandro went toe to toe, the veins in Chase's neck pulsating. She sighed. "Though he doesn't have a chicken neck." She watched as he gestured with his muscular arms, threatening to wring the director's neck. "Or chicken wings."

This wasn't going to end well, she thought, but then Shayonne stepped in, employing her secret weapon. Tears flowed from the reality star's eyes as she implored Chase to allow Alejandro to shoot his 'home movie' so the family could forever cherish Shana's memory. Dead puppies again. She could see Chase's resolve weaken under the onslaught. Oh, man. This was brutal.

"Weird," said Max, commenting on the scene.

"So weird," she agreed. "So what did Clarice say?"

And as Max filled her in, she wondered how she was going to convey this information to Chase. They were now looking for a blood-soaked black robe and a meat cleaver. Only she couldn't tell him. She stroked Max's fur and he purred softly. "You're getting raw meat tonight, buddy. You did good."

"But I thought you said it was too expensive."

"This is a special occasion. You just helped solve a murder."

"Thanks, Odelia," he murmured.

"You're welcome." They watched as Chase caved. Shalonda Kenspeckle had shown up. She was the spitting image of

Shayonne, only her long, dark hair sported red highlights. She was rocking a clingy white top and a miniskirt. Very stylish. Now both sisters were crying their eyes out. There's only so much a man can bear, and soon the cameraman was hoisting the camera onto his shoulder with a triumphant flourish and filming resumed.

Chase came stumbling out of the house, looking sandbagged.

"What the hell just happened?" he asked as he took a seat next to Odelia.

"Welcome to reality TV, Detective," she said. "Try to keep up."

Chapter 7

While Odelia and Chase tried to take control of the crime scene, Dooley, Harriet, Brutus and I were busy trying to figure out what else we could do to solve this murder case. Clarice had pulled one of her disappearing acts again and had vanished like a puff of smoke. Typical. One minute she was there, the next she was gone. And without even bothering to say goodbye.

"Are you really going to share your meat with her?" Harriet asked.

"Sure," said Brutus. "At least until I solve this murder. The moment I catch the killer she can kiss her meat goodbye." I noticed the big bully sounded a lot more macho now that Clarice wasn't there to keep him in line.

"Why would Clarice kiss her meat goodbye?" asked Dooley. "Wouldn't she just eat it?"

"It's an expression," I told him.

"It doesn't make any sense. Why kiss your meat goodbye?"

"Oh, Dooley," said Harriet with a sigh.

"Yes?" he asked, looking up.

"Just go away."

"Go away? Go where?"

"Anywhere. Just stop asking stupid questions."

I patted my friend on the back. "It's all right, Dooley. You know what they say. There are no stupid questions. Only stupid answers."

"I didn't know they said that."

"Well, now you do."

"We should split up," Brutus said. "You and Dooley go this way. Harriet and I will go that way." He was vaguely gesturing toward the house.

"Why?" asked Dooley, remembering there are no stupid questions.

"I've got a better chance cracking this case than you two losers. Isn't that right, sugar pie?"

The sugar pie bit wasn't directed at either me or Dooley. It was meant for Harriet, who fluttered her eyelashes. "Of course I agree, honey bunch. With your intellect and my charm I'm sure we'll crack this case right open."

I eyed Brutus suspiciously. "You've got a theory, haven't you?"

"You bet your whiskers I do. I'm surprised you don't. It's staring you right in the face."

Dooley looked around. "What's staring us in the face?"

"Oh, Dooley," said Harriet, rolling her eyes.

"Look, whatever you think you know, I'm Odelia's cat, so I'm the one who helps her solve the murder. So you better tell me what you know."

Brutus grinned. "Not this time, Maxie baby. This time we're doing things different." He tapped his chest, like a miniature King Kong. "I'm going to solve this case. And I'm going to make sure Odelia knows it."

I shook my head. "You can't do that. That's not fair."

Harriet shrugged. "I think it's time you learned to share, Max. You've had Odelia all to yourself for far too long. It's time to share her with Brutus."

"But-but-but," I sputtered. I caught Brutus's eye and I could tell he was enjoying himself. For the first time since he arrived in town he had me licked.

"That's not very nice of you," said Dooley. "Odelia is Max's human."

Harriet walked up to him. "Odelia is our human, Dooley. She cares about all of us. You. Me. Max. And now Brutus. We're one big happy family."

She sold it so well I almost bought it. But Odelia knew all about Brutus's habit of bossing us around. She'd never accept him into our home if I didn't want to. So maybe I didn't have to worry. Even if he solved the murder first, Odelia would still love me the most. Right?

I watched Brutus and Harriet stalk off. "You're right, Dooley," I said.

"I am?" he asked, surprised.

"It's not very nice of Harriet to take Brutus's side like that."

"So she's not our friend anymore?"

"She is, but she's strayed from the path of true friendship." I shook my head. "Somehow we're going to have to show her the error of her ways."

"I have no idea what you just said, but I think you're probably right."

"Let's just do what we do best and find ourselves a killer."

"All right," he said with a yawn. "But maybe we'll take a nap first?"

"No napping," I said decidedly. "First we catch the killer, then we nap."

Dooley sighed. "Oh, all right. So where do we start?"

"We'll just snoop around. Be the perfect spies."

"Pity the Kenspeckles don't have cats. Otherwise this would be a snap."

We both stared at Kane, who was staring back at us from a safe distance. He'd lost his fighting spirit after his scrap with Clarice. Or maybe he was trying to come up with a new strategy to take us down.

We walked to the house, and the French Bulldog disappeared from sight. Whatever his strategy was, he wasn't taking any chances. I saw that the director of the Kenspeckle show was instructing his cameraman about what to shoot next. The two sisters, Shayonne and Shalonda, having shot their scenes, were being fussed over by a makeup person. A stylist pecked at the hem of Shalonda's skirt, which had silver sequins snaking down the sides.

"Must be nice to have someone fussing over you like that," said Dooley.

"I doubt it. I for one wouldn't want anyone telling me what to wear."

"That's easy for you to say. You're a cat. You don't wear anything."

"You're a cat too," I reminded him. "You don't wear anything either."

"Oh. Right." He looked surprised. "Pity."

"Pity you don't get to wear clothes? Why? I'll bet it's a big fuss."

"Not if you're a Kenspeckle. They have people fussing over the fuss."

And we were right back where we started. "Why would you even want to wear clothes? Or have someone fussing over you?"

"Why wouldn't I? Just imagine having your own personal groomer. Someone to take care of your fur twenty-four seven. Or a personal dietician."

He had a point. It sure would be nice to be pampered and spoiled and treated like a Kenspeckle. Not that Odelia doesn't take good care of me, but she's pretty pressed for time most of the time, with that job of hers and all.

Dooley sighed wistfully. "Wouldn't it be nice to be human for a change?"

That was taking it too far. "No way! I would never want to be human."

"Why not?"

"Uh-uh. Too much stress. Imagine having to work for a living, so you can pay for a roof over your head and food on your table. What a nightmare. And then there's the IRS to deal with and the electric company and the insurance people. I think us cats have the best deal. All we do is sleep a lot, rub our human's legs from time to time, look cute doing it and they pay the rent, the electric bill, the medical bill... All so we can focus on the important stuff."

"Like sleeping and eating."

"No. All of that frees up time to think."

He stared at me. "Think? Think about what?"

"Well, this case for instance. Who killed Shana Kenspeckle."

"Riiight." It was obvious I lost him. Dooley is not exactly a big thinker. In fact, apart from eating and sleeping, I don't think he's got a lot on his mind. Except Harriet, of course. The cat's obsessed with Harriet for some reason. No idea why. I would never get that obsessed over a female. It's degrading.

We watched as the body of Shana was carted off on a stretcher. The coroner had done his bit and stood conferring with Chase. Odelia was keeping an eye on Shayonne and Shalonda who were still being prepped.

"They don't show a lot of emotion between takes," Dooley said.

"They probably reserve all of it for when the cameras are rolling."

"Weird."

"Totally."

I caught a glimpse of Brutus and Harriet, sneaking into the house, and I nudged Dooley. "We better get a move on. Or else Brutus will beat us to it."

He started. "Brutus is going to beat us?"

"Oh, Dooley."

Chapter 8

"I'm starting to think they're all guilty."

"How do you figure?"

"Shayonne told me the murder is the best thing that could have happened to them."

Chase's eyebrows rose. "She said that?"

"Yep. The show's been dropping in the ratings, and the murder will turn that around. Put them right back on top."

"That's just cold."

"Which is why I think they might have set this up together."

"You mean the whole family is in on this?"

"That's exactly what I think. They needed to salvage their show so they decided to sacrifice one of them." Now that she spoke the words out loud, it sounded a bit far-fetched. Still, it was a plausible theory. Fairly plausible.

"That's just crazy, Poole."

Or not.

"The Kenspeckles might be a little dysfunctional, but they're not killers."

She watched as the cameras started rolling again. On cue, Shayonne and Shalonda broke down in tears, clutching at each other for support.

"A little dysfunctional?" she asked.

"Well, maybe a lot dysfunctional. But that doesn't make them killers."

"So what's next?" She had no idea how to conduct a police investigation. This was the first time she was on the inside, not on the outside looking in.

"I got a message from your uncle just before," Chase said. "He's cutting his vacation short and will be back tomorrow."

"What? He was looking forward to that fishing trip."

"The mayor is considering calling in the FBI so he needs to be here to convince him otherwise."

She made a mental eye roll. "The FBI? This is a local investigation."

"Apparently the Kenspeckles are considered a national treasure."

She watched as Shayonne and Shalonda stood hamming it up in front of the camera and shook her head. "Some national treasure."

He grinned. "There's that sarcasm again."

"Nope. Like I said, I don't do sarcasm. Not me."

"Let's see if your uncle can persuade the mayor to keep the FBI out of this. First things first: we need to set up interviews with everyone involved."

"What about the note?"

"What about it?"

"What does it say?"

He slipped his iPhone from his back pocket and showed her a snapshot of the note. "We fed it into Google Translate and it spat out this message."

She took his phone and read out loud, "You deserve to die, Shana Kenspeckle. You are dog excrement. In fact you're less than dog excrement. You're the fly on dog excrement. In fact you're the excrement from the fly on dog excrement. Or the ameba on the fly's excrement." It went on like this for a while. The final sentence read, "Hellfire will rain down on you and your filthy brood. This is just the beginning." She handed him back his phone. "I guess the killer is not a big Kenspeckle fan."

"The fact that these phrases came out in perfect English means the original message was written in English and then translated with Google Translate. Otherwise only gobbledygook would have come out. Which means—"

"This was a pretty feeble attempt to make it look like a terrorist attack."

He smiled. "Which tells us the killer isn't a professional."

She wondered whether to tell him they were looking for a blood-splattered black robe and mask. But since she couldn't tell him about the robe without revealing her secret, she decided to keep mum. It didn't matter anyway, as Clarice hadn't gotten a look at the killer's face.

Chase headed for the bedroom and she followed him. She stared down at the bed. The coroner's people had stripped the sheets for evidence but had left the stained mattress. "The killer was smart," Chase said. "Abe found traces of chloroform in all the bedrooms. All the Kenspeckles were drugged."

"What about the film crew?"

"Nope. Not a trace. But since they're staying at the guest house and aren't allowed in the main house when shooting wraps that wasn't necessary."

"They're not allowed inside the house?"

"The Kenspeckles have strict rules about it. They cherish their privacy."

"Except when they don't. Like when they share every private moment with a worldwide audience."

He smiled. "Ah, but they only show you what they want you to see."

She nodded. "So did you check the rooms for prints?" Dumb question. The guy was a bonafide detective. And the killer had probably worn gloves.

"Well, we tried, but the Kenspeckles gave us a lot of lip. Any normal family would have canceled their trip, moved to a hotel until they could catch a flight home, and given us free reign to search the place top to bottom. But the sisters are adamant to stay here and finish the shoot."

"They're giving you a hard time."

"They sure are. And I don't even know why. It's almost as if they don't want us to find the killer." When she opened her mouth to speak, he said, "And don't give me that 'The whole family is in on this' nonsense, Poole."

She quickly closed her mouth again. No, that was just a crazy theory.

She glanced at the window, where Clarice must have been watching the killer. Chills ran down her spine. What a horrible scene to watch. A thought occurred to her. "The killer must have known his way around the place."

Chase nodded, a sparkle in his eye. "Uh-huh."

"He also knew the film crew would never set foot inside the house after filming was finished for the day. And he also had access to the house."

"Go on."

She smiled. "This was an inside job. The killer was either a family member or security personnel. They were the only ones with access."

"Your uncle Alec was right," he said with a grin. "You're pretty astute."

"Watch me. I'll catch this killer before you can say 'fly excrement.'"

"Fly excrement."

"Smart-ass."

Chapter 9

Dooley and I searched around for the best vantage point. It had to be clean and comfy, and it had to be high enough so we could have a great view. I caught sight of a fabulous beige crocodile couch. I felt bad for the crocodiles that had lost life and hide, but the couch was easily the best spot in the room, affording 360 vision and a soft, flat surface. It was exactly what we needed. I gave Dooley a nudge and we both hopped up onto the couch, clambered over about a million embroidered throw pillows and settled on the head rest.

All the main principals were gathered on the deck for an impromptu meeting, and Dooley and I settled in to watch. Don't look so shocked. We're cats. Lying around and spying on humans is what we do. It had also crossed my mind that there was probably some yummy food to be found in this place, and from here we could look straight into the kitchen. I was pretty sure Kane got the best food money could buy, and I wanted me some of that.

Us cats might not like dogs, but we like to steal their food just fine.

"Look, Max," said Dooley, pointing to the kitchen. Brutus was chasing Kane, and the dog was doing his utmost to stay out of his clutches.

"Looks like Brutus is trying to talk to Kane," I said lazily. After all this traipsing around I was starting to feel the strain, and I was ready for a nap. I know I'd told Dooley we'd nap once we caught the killer, but the couch was so comfy, and the sun on our furs so nice and warm, I was feeling drowsy.

"I wonder what that's all about," said Dooley with a cavernous yawn.

"Probably something to do with his so-called theory."

Brutus always has theories, usually pretty far-fetched. We had another murder not so long ago, when a famous eighties pop singer was killed. Brutus thought things through and came up with the theory that the guy had been killed by a conspiracy of boy toys. He probably thought a confederacy of French Bulldogs had killed Shana Kenspeckle and Kane was the ring leader.

"I don't think we need to worry about Brutus cracking this case," I said.

I returned my attention to the Kenspeckles, who were concluding their meeting. Shayonne was there, and Shalonda, and of course Shayonne's husband Dion, and Shana's husband Damien LeWood. They were discussing things with Alejandro Salanova, the director, and some of the other crew members. I also saw a bodyguard hovering nearby, pressing a finger to his ear from time to time and looking decidedly shifty-eyed. A barber had had fun with his facial hair, which ran in three parallel lines from his lips to his ears, where it morphed into a butter-colored buzzcut, and he was rocking golden hoops. He reminded me of the Genie in Disney's Aladdin, without the blue body paint. And the grin. This guy had never cracked a smile in his life.

"I think they're going to start filming again," said Dooley.

"Well, they have to strike while the iron is hot, I suppose," I said. Everybody would want to know what happened, and who better to inform them than the Kenspeckles themselves? Regular families would probably mourn in silence. The Kenspeckles filmed another episode of their show.

"It's that old saying," said Dooley. "The show must move on."

"Go on."

"But I just got here."

"No, I mean the show."

"What about it?"

"The show must go on."

"That's what I said."

"No, you said... Forget about it."

"Forget about the show?"

"It doesn't matter, Dooley."

Once again, Brutus came shooting past us, chasing Kane, who was now running for his life. He probably thought Brutus was going to cut him, like Clarice had. Brutus took a breather, glaring up at us. "Do I have to do all the work around here? Why don't you two lazy bums give me a paw already?"

"You said you wanted to split up, remember? Split up into teams."

He made a throwaway gesture with his paw. "Gah. Fuggedaboutit."

We watched him stalk off again, muttering something under his breath. It didn't sound very friendly. I didn't care. It was fun to watch Brutus run around like a headless chicken. I'd never seen a cat chase a dog before, and the sight was both disturbing and highly entertaining.

Odelia and Chase came walking into the living room and Odelia gave us a wink. I tried to wink back, but cat's eyes aren't made for winking, so it probably came off weird. She got the message, though: we were on the case.

Just then, a person pointing a camera came crashing through the privacy hedge lining the deck and pool area. He looked a little crazed and hyped up.

"Paparazzi alert," I told Dooley.

"Oh, is that a paparazzi?" he asked, interested.

"Paparazzo. They only call them paparazzi when they travel in packs."

The moment the photog caught sight of the Kenspeckle sisters, he started clicking his camera, firing off questions like a machine gun toting kook.

"Shayonne! Shayonne! Where were you when your sister was killed?!"

Highly inappropriate, I felt. Genie the Bodyguard felt the same way, for he tried to swat the pap like a bug. The photographer dove under Genie's massive arm and just kept shooting like the nasty little shutterbug he was.

"Is it true that Shana was sleeping with your husband, Shayonne?!"

The paparazzo narrowly avoided a flying tackle and darted away in the direction of the pool, the bodyguard close on his heel and moving in.

"Is this the end of the Kenspeckles?! The final nail in your coffin?!"

"Wow. That's just plain mean," said Dooley.

We watched the bodyguard zoom in on the pap. Amazingly, the scrawny pap kept on firing his camera. Courage under fire. Or the smell of money.

"For a guy built like a freight train that bodyguard sure moves fast," Dooley said.

"I think he's going to catch him. I think he's going to catch him and sit on his head and squash him like a melon."

But then the reporter lost his footing and splashed headfirst into the pool.

"Aw," both Dooley and I said. Talk about a downer ending.

I was starting to feel like those two old guys on *The Muppet Show*, Statler and Waldorf, keeping up a running commentary. And I was starting to understand the appeal of the Kenspeckles. They sure knew how to put on a good show. You never knew what was going to happen next.

The bodyguard plucked the photog from the pool and dragged him ashore. He looked like a drowned chicken, spluttering and yelling his head off. He was still holding on to his camera, though, and was clicking away.

"You have to hand it to him," Dooley said. "He's one dedicated dude."

The bodyguard started frogmarching the intruder off the premises. Just then, Kane came racing past, followed by a panting Brutus. They slipped between the bodyguard's feet, and he toppled into the pool, dragging the paparazzo with him, making a big splash. The spray spattered all the way to Shayonne and Shalonda Kenspeckle, who shouted their annoyance. They used words I'd never heard before. Very original. And very colorful.

"Man, they've got dirty mouths," said Dooley, looking shocked.

"They'll probably cut that from the show. Have to keep it PG."

The bodyguard and the paparazzo came splashing from the pool, both soaking wet, the bodyguard's face a thundercloud. The man was seriously pissed. Just then, more paparazzi came crashing through the boxwood hedge, and suddenly we were at a full-blown red-carpet event, cameras clicking and people shouting and clamoring for attention. More bodyguards came rushing to the scene, trying to catch the out-of-control paps.

"This is so much fun!" Dooley cried.

There were paparazzi everywhere, chased by burly rent-a-cops. A few more paps ended up in the pool while others were pinned to the deck. In the middle of all this pandemonium, Brutus was still chasing Kane, though the chase had slowed down to a crawl as both were running out of gas now.

"I'm starting to like the Kenspeckles," I said. "Great entertainment value."

"Yeah, me too," said Dooley. "Ouch." The exclamation was in reference to more paparazzi tripping over Brutus and Kane. They were tackling more paps than the bodyguards were. Maybe the Kenspeckles should appoint Brutus to head up their security team. He was doing some serious damage.

"Looks like Brutus is scoring one for the home team," I said.

Harriet had jumped up on the couch and was watching the scene intently.

"Shouldn't you be helping your boyfriend?" Dooley asked a little bitterly.

I didn't blame him. Us cats might not be on Facebook but that doesn't mean we like it when someone unfriends us the way Harriet had done.

"I don't know what's gotten into him," Harriet said, shaking her head sadly. "He's got this cockamamie theory about the murder, and he's adamant that Kane is going to supply him with the missing link to the killer."

"What's his theory?" I asked.

She hesitated, loyalty to her boyfriend warring with her desire to unburden her soul. Finally the need to confide in someone won out. "He thinks Shana was killed by a giant dog who bit her head off."

I stared at her, dumbfounded. I hadn't expected this.

"A giant dog?" asked Dooley. "You mean like a big, humongous dog?"

She frowned at him. "Yeah, a gigantic dog who bit her head off and spit it out again when he discovered he didn't like the taste of human head after all."

"That's crazy," Dooley said. "The Kenspeckles don't have a giant dog."

I stared at Dooley. "Is that what you think is crazy here? What about the idea that dogs bite people's heads off?"

"Well, don't they?" he asked.

"Of course they don't! It's a physical impossibility!"

"But what if they're big enough? Like Cujo?"

"Cujo never bit anybody's head off! No dog can bite someone's head off!"

"Well, Brutus is convinced they can," said Harriet. "He's convinced the Kenspeckles have a pack of vicious dogs running around. He's seen them on one of those Bravo shows. Huge and ferocious creatures. All the big-name celebrities keep them nowadays. To protect themselves from paparazzi and kidnappers and stalkers. He thinks one of the dogs went rogue. Got a taste for human blood and bit Shana's head clean off. And now the Kenspeckles are trying to cover it up. They're hiding the dog somewhere in this house. He thinks Kane knows where, and he's trying to get him to give up the location."

"To get him to roll over on his monster dog friend?" I asked.

She nodded, chewing her lip. "He says he needs to break Kane. Make him squeal on his canine brother. Says it's the only way to get the truth."

"But what about Clarice's statement? What about the masked killer and the big-ass meat cleaver?" I asked, exasperated.

"Brutus says Clarice can't be trusted. She's nuts and will say whatever to get attention. And his meat. She'll do anything for a slice of filet mignon."

"Your boyfriend is crazy," Dooley said. "Absolutely batshit crazy."

Well, I wouldn't have put it so strongly, but basically he was right.

"At least we don't have to worry about Brutus getting in good with Odelia," I said. "If he tries to sell her his mad dog theory she'll just laugh."

"Oh, cut it out, Max," said Harriet, giving me an angry look.

"Cut out what? What are you talking about?"

"Cut out the bullying. You've been mean to Brutus from the start."

I couldn't believe what she was saying. "Me? Mean to him?"

"Yes, you are a mean cat and a bully. Can't you see that Brutus wants to fit in? To be welcomed into the community? He's doing his best and you keep pushing him away. I think it's very selfish of you, Max. You too, Dooley."

This was just crazy talk. "Look, he's the one who started bossing us around from the moment he set foot in this town."

"Can't you see through that, Max? That's just a pose. Deep down, Brutus is a gentle, sensitive soul. All he wants is to be loved and accepted the way he is." She sighed as we all watched Brutus chasing Kane around the pool.

"Come back here, you little weasel!" he was shouting. "Wait till I get my claws on you, you stupid mutt!"

Harriet was right. A gentle and sensitive soul. No doubt about it.

More and more paparazzi were splashing in the pool, tripped up by Brutus and Kane, and had to be fished out by bodyguards. Who knew so many paps couldn't swim? Brutus was doing the Kenspeckles a big favor.

"I don't see it," said Dooley. "I don't see the sensitive side in Brutus."

"Well, he's got one," Harriet snapped. "You're not looking hard enough."

Dooley opened his mouth to retort. When he caught Harriet's eye he thought better of it and closed it again. There are some battles you can't win.

"Brutus is the sweetest cat you can imagine," she said. "A real gentlecat."

"I'm going to cut you, you ugly mongrel!" the gentlecat was screaming. "I'm going to cut you up so bad even your own mother won't recognize you!"

"The only reason he behaves like this is because..." She sighed, and fixed me with an accusatory look. "Because he wants to impress you, Max."

"Impress me!" I cried.

"Of course. Why else do you think he keeps challenging you? Secretly Brutus looks up to you. You're his hero. All he wants is to be like you."

I shook my head. "This is just... I can't even..."

"Look at yourself, Max. You've got it all! You've got the best human in Hampton Cove. You've got a great home. Great friends. You're even an ace detective. You've got it all." She gave me a pleading look. "Is it so hard to believe Brutus wants to be a part of that? That he wants to be your friend?"

"Yes, it's very hard to believe," Dooley said.

"Well, it's the truth," she snapped. "And if you can't see that, then who's the bully here?" She stalked away, tail high. We both stared after her.

"You don't believe a word she said, do you?" Dooley asked. "All that talk about Brutus just wanting to be your friend? That's just a bunch of hooey."

"Of course I don't," I said. "She loves the cat. She'll believe anything."

We watched Harriet chasing Brutus chasing Kane for a while.

"Do you think this evil dog theory holds water, Max?"

"Absolutely not," I said. "I believe Clarice. Whoever killed Shana was wearing a black robe and a mask, and whoever was beneath that robe definitely wasn't a killer dog. Unless dogs can walk on their hind legs and handle a meat cleaver." Before Dooley could reply, I quickly added, "Which they can't."

The Kenspeckles were also staring at the scene, commenting freely, while the cameraman filmed the whole thing. This was going to be the gag reel for their next show. Some comic relief after the horror of the murder.

But even as the circus was in full swing, I didn't forget for one moment that one of these people was a killer. Was it Shayonne? Shalonda? Dion Dread? Damien LeWood? I saw that both Odelia and Chase were watching the foursome intently, and I knew they were wondering the same thing.

Outside, the bodyguards snatched up the last of the paparazzi, escorting them off the premises. Kane, desperate to escape Brutus, had thought of nothing better than to jump into the pool, right on top of the head of the head bodyguard, who was wrestling three paparazzi. Brutus was stumped. He wanted to get a hold of Kane, but he drew the line at jumping into the pool. Us cats don't like to swim. It's not that we can't swim—that's a common misconception. It's just that we prefer not to. It's all because of our furry coats. We swell up like a sponge. It just makes us look ridiculous.

So Brutus just sat there, staring daggers at Kane, while Kane sat on top of the bodyguard's head, making faces at Brutus. Classic standoff.

"Well, looks like the show's over," said Dooley, sounding disappointed.

"Au contraire," I said. "It's just getting started."

Chapter 10

The last of the paparazzi had been caught and thrown off the property, but not before Shayonne and Shalonda had hit their marks and struck their poses, giving them what they came for. You don't get to be in the world's top-rated reality show without giving back to the fans. Kane the dog had been fished from the pool, and it was time to finally sit down for the interview.

The sisters refused to be interviewed separately and Chase decided not to fight them on this. What he did fight them on was their expressed desire that the entire interview was filmed for their show. What was more, they wanted the murder investigation taped, Chase and Odelia included for this special.

They'd even get screen credit and SAG minimum, whatever that was.

Chase vehemently refused, and so did Odelia, though less vehemently. She wouldn't mind being on national TV. Her mom would freak if she saw her daughter strutting her stuff amongst all these celebs. But Chase muttered something about making a mockery of the investigation and that was that.

"Not gonna happen," were his exact words, and no matter how much the sisters insisted, even turning on the waterworks again, this time he stood his ground. He obviously had no aspirations to be a celebrity cop.

Shalonda tossed her long hair. “You know what we’ll do, Shayonne?”

“What?”

“We’ll shoot a confessional. Tell our viewers all about the investigation. They can’t stop us from doing that, can they?”

Both sisters gave Chase an inquisitive look, but he just shook his head.

The sisters had chosen the pergola for the interview. The wooden structure, covered with vines and honeysuckle, stood fifty yards from the house, at the bottom of the garden, providing a nice view of the Atlantic Ocean. Dappled sunlight slanted down through the rafters, and as far as Odelia could see there were no paparazzi in sight. What she did see was the cameraman sneaking around, trying to get the best view of the sisters.

She decided not to tell Chase. This was a fight they couldn’t win.

The Kenspeckles made themselves comfortable on the wicker furniture, making sure the camera caught them from their best angle. Even during a police interview they were concerned about how they looked on camera.

In a surprising shift of protocol, Chase had decided to allow Odelia to take the lead in the interview. Maybe he figured Shayonne and Shalonda would open up to her more than to him. More so because she didn’t look anything like a cop. In fact she might have featured on the show herself.

“Did Shana have any enemies?” she asked, opening the interview.

“Oh, no,” Shalonda said immediately. “Shana was the most beloved person on earth. Literally everyone adored her. I mean, literally every single person on earth loved Shana to bits. I'm not kidding. I know this for a fact."

"Yeah, Shana was a sweetheart," Shayonne agreed. "She had the biggest heart. You could never hope to have a sweeter sister than her." A tear stole down her cheek, and Shalonda reached out a hand and gave hers a squeeze.

Faced with tragedy, the Kenspeckle sisters offered a united front. It was touching, Odelia thought. Until she saw movement from the corner of her eye, and noticed the camera recording every last second of the teary scene.

"Can you think of anyone who would have wanted to cause her harm?"

Shayonne hesitated. "Well, there was this one incident with one of her ex-boyfriends, Robin Masters. When Shana got engaged to Damien, he made a big scene. I mean, the guy completely lost it. Went absolutely ballistic."

"Oh, that's right. Wasn't that in season ten? Or was it eleven? I forget."

"It was so horrible," said Shayonne. "Robin drove up to the house and threatened to torch the place. Camille—that's our mother, Camille Kenspeckle—had to intervene and calm him down. The cops got involved, and Shana had to file a restraining order against the guy. I was terrified."

"He wasn't the only one. There have been others. Other ex-boyfriends. But they're usually pretty amenable once they get their five minutes of fame."

"You mean fifteen minutes of fame," Odelia said.

"What's that, honey?" asked Shalonda. "You have to speak up, for the—"

But before she could say 'microphone,' Shayonne had squeezed her hand.

"The expression is fifteen minutes of fame, not five," Odelia explained.

"Oh, but these guys only get five," said Shalonda. "We're the stars of the show. Bit players like Robin Masters don't get to steal our limelights."

"They sure don't," Shayonne agreed. "We worked too damn hard. No boyfriend gets first billing. Five minutes and that's it. It's all in the contract."

"Does everybody sign a contract?" asked Odelia.

"Of course," said Shayonne. "Girlfriends, boyfriends, husbands, wives… Camille takes care of all of that. This is a business, honey. We need to protect the Kenspeckle brand. Nobody is going to come and mess with our brand."

"And what is that brand, exactly?" Chase asked, unable to control himself.

"Beauty and grace," said Shayonne instantly, as if she'd rehearsed the phrase, which she probably had.

"Wealth and power," added Shalonda.

"Style and beauty."

"I think you said beauty twice, honey," said Shalonda.

"That's because it's important. The Kenspeckle brand is all about beauty."

"And selfies," Odelia said with a smile.

The two sisters laughed. "You said it, girl," said Shalonda.

"Wasn't Shana called the queen of selfies?" asked Odelia. "Maybe her habit of portraying her wealth and beauty made some people feel jealous?"

"Oh, but everybody was jealous of her," Shayonne confirmed. "Shana was so gorgeous it was hard not to feel jealous. She was the center of attention wherever she went. I'll admit even I felt jealous of her from time to time."

"Yeah, she couldn't walk into a room without getting everyone to turn."

"Remember my wedding? How she upstaged me in front of everybody? That dress. That hair. She looked like she was the one getting married."

"I hated her for that," said Shalonda.

"Me too. Or that time when I was sixteen, going out on my first date and she was flirting with my date? The guy didn't even look at me after that!"

"Shana was an attention whore, no doubt about it," said Shalonda. "And we all loved her for it," she quickly added when she saw Chase frown.

"She was the most popular star in the family, wasn't she?" asked Odelia.

The two sisters stared at her, momentarily lost for words. Then Shayonne asked, "Who the hell told you that?"

"That's not true," Shalonda chimed in.

"We're all stars. Just look at our contracts. We all get star credit."

"There's no denying Shana got the most attention," said Chase. "She got the endorsement deals, the paid appearances... Even her app is a bestseller."

Wow. Chase had obviously done his homework.

"Those are just rumors," Shayonne said, sitting up.

"Filthy lies," Shalonda chimed in, also sitting up.

"We all share equal billing on our show. There are no prima donnas."

"Still," Chase insisted. "You just said you hated your sister because she upstaged you, and tried to steal your boyfriends."

"Oh, she did," said Shayonne, nodding.

"She most definitely did," Shalonda agreed.

"Which doesn't mean we didn't love her."

"Oh, yeah. We loved her to pieces."

"Tiny, little pieces," said Shayonne, holding her nails millimeters apart.

"You told me that Shana was sleeping with your husband?" Odelia asked.

"You told her that?" asked Shalonda, turning to her sister. "What about putting up a united front for the outside world, like Camille told us to? Family first, Shayonne. Family always comes first."

"This is a police investigation," Chase reminded her. "You can speak freely. Nothing you say will go beyond Miss Poole and myself at this point."

"All we want is to catch your sister's killer," Odelia assured them.

"Yes, I told her," Shayonne said. "Because it's true. Shana was sleeping with Dion. She told me so herself. She came clean to me last week."

"I don't believe this," Shalonda said, shaking her head. Whether she didn't believe that Shana had been sleeping with Dion or that her sister was confiding in the police wasn't immediately clear. Odelia suspected the latter.

"Well, she was!" Shayonne exclaimed. "She finally confessed. Told me she couldn't live with the lie anymore. She also told me she was done with Dion."

"And how did you react?" asked Chase.

"I was stunned. Completely stunned. And then I dumped Dion's ass."

Odelia frowned. "So why is Dion still here?"

"Because Shana confessed to me off camera, and I broke up with Dion off camera. We needed to do it again, on camera, which is why we all flew out here, because this was going to be the highlight of the season. We were going to end on a big cliffhanger, with my relationship with Shana and my marriage in the balance." She shook her head. "You obviously still have a lot to learn about TV, honey. This all happened already, and now we have to recreate it."

"So Dion was only hanging around until you filmed the bit about the breakup?" asked Chase.

"Well, duh. We were going to milk this thing for all we could get."

"What about Dion? How did he feel about this situation?" Odelia asked.

"Well, he's not too happy," said Shayonne. "He's off the show, isn't he?"

"You snooze, you lose," said Shalonda.

"I don't think that's correct, honey," said Shayonne. "More like, you cheat, you lose."

"It doesn't have the same ring to it. I like mine better."

"What it all comes down to, Detective," said Shayonne, touching Chase's knee, "is that when you cheat on a Kenspeckle you're out on your ass."

"Amen to that," said Shalonda.

Odelia shared a glance with Chase. This was definitely motivation for murder. If Dion was going to get kicked off the show, he stood to lose a lot of money. He might have wanted to plot revenge against Shana. Maybe even hoped that the murder would sink the entire show.

"What about Damien?" asked Chase.

Shayonne swatted away a fly. "What about him?"

"Did he know about Shana and Dion?"

"Of course he did. We don't keep secrets in this family. Damien knew all about his wife's infidelities."

"Infidelities?" asked Odelia. "You mean this wasn't a one-time thing?"

"Nope," said Shayonne. "Now don't get me wrong. Shana was the sweetest person in the world."

"So sweet."

"And I loved her, like, a lot."

"A whole lot."

"But let's not kid ourselves. She was a skank."

"They didn't get any skankier than Shana."

"She never met a guy she didn't want to sleep with and who didn't want to sleep with her." She shrugged. "That's the way she was. Take it or leave it."

"Damien knew that going in," said Shalonda. "In fact he sleeps around just as much as she does. They have a, quote unquote, arrangement."

"So he was fine with this Dion situation?" Odelia asked.

The two sisters shared a look. "Well, fine would be overstating it," said Shayonne.

"Yeah, he and Dion got into a big fight about it the other night."

"They knocked the shit out of each other and then bonded over a couple of beers and hung out at the pool all night. It was crazy."

"Dion is crazy."

"Hey. Who you calling crazy? That's my husband you're talking about."

"Ex-husband," Shalonda specified.

"He's not my ex-husband. I haven't divorced him yet."

Shalonda stared at her sister. "You're not seriously thinking about keeping him, are you? After what he did to you?"

"But I still love him, honey. And maybe now that Shana's gone we can start over."

"You're officially crazy. That man never treated you right."

"He has. And anyway, better to have a man than no man at all."

Shalonda's eyebrows rose and she planted a hand on her hip. "Don't hold back, honey. Just throw it all out there, why don't you?"

"I'm saying you don't get to give me marriage advice. I'm only going to take marriage advice from a person who's in a successful marriage. And that person obviously isn't you."

"I would have had a successful marriage if Shana hadn't stolen my man."

"She wouldn't have stolen your man if he wasn't ready to be stolen."

"Wait, you also had a man stolen from you by Shana?" Odelia asked. She was feeling as if she was on an episode of the Kenspeckles. Which she was.

"Of course. Didn't you listen to a word we said? Shana stole all of our men. That's what she did. She was a man-stealer."

Chase shook his head and jotted something down in his notebook. It wasn't hard to figure out what. Both Shalonda and Shayonne had a motive for murder. Both of them had had their men stolen by their sister.

"Did you notice anything about the intruder last night?" Odelia asked, deciding to change the subject.

"Not a thing," said Shayonne. "I slept like a baby. Though when I woke up I was feeling nauseous. But I already told Detective Kingsley about that."

"You were drugged," Chase confirmed. "Both of you were."

"Yeah, I was feeling nauseous too," said Shalonda. "I thought I was pregnant."

Both sisters laughed. "Good one, Shalonda," said Shayonne.

"What about that?" Odelia asked.

Shalonda blinked. "What about what?"

"Any plans to add a new generation to the Kenspeckle family?"

"Well, Dion and I were planning our first baby," said Shayonne.

"But that's off now, right?" asked Shalonda. When her sister didn't respond, she repeated emphatically, "I said, that's off now. Right?"

Shayonne shrugged.

Shalonda's jaw dropped dramatically. "Oh. My. God. You're not seriously thinking to procreate with that man, are you? He cheated on you with your own sister!"

"That won't happen again," said Shayonne. "He promised."

"Of course it won't happen again! Shana is dead. It's physically impossible for that to happen again. That don't mean he won't do it with some other skank."

"He's a good person," Shayonne insisted. "And it's not because he tripped up once that he should be punished for the rest of his life. He deserves a second chance and I am possibly willing to give him one. Maybe. I'm still thinking."

"Think again! Once a cheater, always a cheater."

"That's not true. He promised he wouldn't do it again and I believe him."

Shalonda raised her eyes to the rafters, as if to draw strength from the honeysuckle. "I'm telling Camille," she finally declared. "I'm so telling her."

Odelia noticed how the cameraman had snuck up on them, and was so caught up in the dramatic scene that he'd dropped all pretenses and was openly filming. This was going to be another cliffhanger, she thought.

"So you didn't notice anything out of the ordinary, apart from the fact that you were both feeling nauseous this morning?" asked Chase, in a heroic effort to take back control of the interview.

"No, Detective," said Shayonne. "I was out like a light all night."

"Me too."

"You are going to catch the killer, right?" asked Shayonne.

"We're going to do everything in our power to find him, ma'am," said Chase. Then he caught sight of the cameraman and cursed loudly.

The cameraman eyed him sheepishly. "Just doing my job, bub."

"Get out of my face," Chase said. "I don't want you anywhere near me."

"Better get used to it," Odelia whispered. "You're a TV detective now."

"Thanks, ladies," he said, ignoring her remark. "That's all for now."

"And it's a wrap," Shayonne cried. "Tell me you got all that?"

The cameraman gave her a toothy grin and a thumbs-up.

"You did great, Detective," Shalonda said. "You're a natural."

"I don't care," he said wearily. "I just want to catch your sister's killer."

"Oh, but so do we," said Shayonne.

"Yeah, that's all we care about," said Shalonda. "Now do you think we could do this again, Detective? Only this time I'll sit there and you sit here."

Chase sighed. "Just... shoot me already. Not you," he said when the cameraman pointed his camera at him. "You shoot me and I'll shoot you."

Yep, this was shaping up to be a pretty interesting murder investigation.

Chapter 11

While Odelia and Chase went off to interview the two leading ladies of Cirque du Kenspeckle, Dooley and I decided to abandon our perch and do some more snooping around. Earn our kibble, if you know what I mean.

The big advantage of being a cat is that we're pretty much invisible. We can stalk around and people will simply pat our heads and go on discussing their latest killing spree or plot a fresh massacre without a care in the world. That's why we're the world's best spies. Well, flies would make even better spies, I suppose, as they can, you know, buzz around from suspect to suspect. But I've never heard of a fly living long enough to tell its tale to its human owner. Even supposing flies have human owners, of course, which I don't think they have. Flies don't provide as much warmth and affection as cats do.

We wandered about the house, and our first port of call was the kitchen. I think we were both curious to see what kind of food Kane was being fed.

The kitchen was an all-white, very spacious affair, with a gigantic butcher block in the center, and all the usual gleaming appliances occupying the enormous space. You could film a cooking show here. Maybe they did. We followed our noses, and padded into what looked like a mudroom, with coats on racks and boots neatly placed beneath them. And there it was: a placemat with two large bowls. We eagerly trotted up, and I have to say I was disappointed to find both bowls empty. Fortunately for Kane the Kenspeckles had invested in a Drinkwell. I wasn't thirsty, though, and neither was Dooley.

"No food?" he asked.

"Looks like."

"How is that even possible?!"

I was starting to feel sorry for the annoying little yapper. First his human was murdered by some maniac with a meat cleaver, then he'd been attacked by a feral cat, and chased around the pool by a violent intruder, and now, to add insult to injury, the Kenspeckles had forgotten to feed him.

"Looks like Kane has a lot to complain about," said Dooley.

"Yeah, a thing like this would never happen in our home."

We shared a look of understanding. Odelia's place might not be the palatial house the Kenspeckles could afford, but at least she'd never forgotten to feed us, and neither had her mom or Gran. In that sense, we had it made.

"Come to gloat?" suddenly a raspy voice asked.

We turned in surprise, and saw that Kane sat glaring at us.

"Oh, no," I said. "Far from it. Just curious to see how the other half lives."

"The other half lives rottenly," he said, and I noticed he spoke with a lisp, as if he had a speech impediment. Or maybe all dogs spoke like that. I wouldn't know. I rarely move in canine circles. I'm strictly a feline person.

"Yeah, I can see that," I said. "They forgot to feed you, didn't they?"

He plunked down on his haunches and stared at us a little wearily.

"Shana used to feed me, but I guess that's over now. She died, you know."

"Yeah, we know," said Dooley.

"That's why we're here," I said. "We're investigating her murder."

"Trying to figure out whodunnit," Dooley added, in case it wasn't clear.

Kane nodded forlornly. "She was a good human. Always bought me the best food and allowed me to sleep on the bed. Took me everywhere, she did. Hong Kong, the Bahamas, Europe... We traveled the world together."

"That's nice," I said, for lack of a better response. I didn't care a hoot about traveling. I'm something of a homebody. Traveling gives me the willies.

"So what happened to your friend?" he asked. "The one that's been chasing me all over the place?"

"Oh, he's not our friend," I hastened to say. "More an acquaintance."

"Brutus has this theory," Dooley said. "He wants you to confirm it."

"Theory? What theory?"

"Well, that your human was killed by a huge, ferocious dog."

"A dog that bit her head off," I added helpfully.

"He thinks the Kenspeckles are hiding this dog in the basement, afraid the police will find out and accuse them of being assassins to murder."

"Accessories," I corrected him. "Accessories to murder."

Kane stared at us for a moment, then frowned. He looked even sadder than usual, and bulldogs have a pretty sad face to begin with. "I always knew cats were nuts," he said. "But now I finally have proof. You two are cuckoo."

"Oh, no. We don't believe any of Brutus's ideas either," said Dooley.

"You don't?" This seemed to surprise the bulldog.

"No, we think he's cuckoo, too," I said. "I mean, no dog can produce a bite force of enough pounds of pressure to sever the human spinal cord." I laughed. "They'd need jaws of steel to accomplish such a feat." Dooley and Kane were staring at me, so I was quick to add, "I watch the Discovery Channel. *MythBusters*? Such a great show. If you're into that kind of thing, of course." Which Dooley and my new canine friend obviously weren't.

"I still don't get what that's got to do with me," said Kane.

"Brutus figures you and this nonexistent Jaws of Steel are buddies, seeing as you're both dogs and all, and he hopes you'll squeal on your chum."

The bulldog's frown deepened, and now he actually looked like Tommy Lee Jones having a bad day. "He's crazy," he said curtly.

"Pretty much our opinion as well," I said.

"He *is* crazy," Dooley confirmed.

"And dangerous. He said he was going to cut me. He's a menace."

"Yeah, well, his meow is worse than his bite," I said.

"If you have to know, I'm the only dog on the premises. There are no other pets allowed in the house—though it's obvious the Kenspeckles are slacking on the rules now that Shana's gone. She always said I was her one and only Kenspeckle prince, and she wanted to keep it that way. She got me endorsement deals, and was prepping me for my own TV show, debuting in the fall. Damien was even designing a collection for me. My own fashion line. He was calling it Kane's Kraze." He sighed and plunked his head down on his paws, looking sad. "All gone now. No Shana. No TV show. No fashion line."

"What about the other Kenspeckles?" I asked, feeling sorry for the dog.

"Yeah, I'll bet they'll adopt you now," said Dooley.

He lifted his shoulders in an almost imperceptible shrug. "I liked Shana. She was the sweetest of the bunch." He licked his snout with his long, pink tongue. "You see what's happening, don't you? The minute Shana's gone they forget about me. I'm going to starve to death in this place. I'll be forced to fend for myself. Forage for food in the Hampton Cove jungle. Survive."

"We don't have a jungle in Hampton Cove," I said. "Only a park."

"And a forest. But that's where Clarice rules," Dooley added.

"The cat that tried to cut you," I clarified.

He groaned. "I'm doomed."

"You're not doomed. You're a celebrity," I said. "You've got fan clubs, an Instagram page, Twitter, Facebook, Snapchat. Literally millions of fans."

"I do? I didn't even know. I guess Shana set all that up in my name."

"What I mean is that you'll be well taken care of. You're an icon, Kane."

This perked him up a little. At least his ears were pointing up again.

"Yeah, the Kenspeckles aren't going to let anything happen to you," Dooley said.

"They almost did. They allowed this crazy cat to chase me around the pool about a billion times and then do a death leap into the pool. Good thing Boa was there, or I might have drowned."

"Boa?" I asked.

"Stanbury Boa. Bodyguard. He runs the security detail that protects the Kenspeckles."

"And he's probably going to get fired," Dooley muttered.

He was right. Bodyguards get fired when the bodies they're hired to guard are found dead. I wondered why the ax hadn't fallen yet on Boa's employment.

"I'm sure they're all a little preoccupied right now," I told Kane. "What with the murder and all. Speaking of murder, we have it from a usually reliable source that you actually witnessed the murder? Is that true?"

He nodded sadly. "Yeah, I was there. And let me tell you, it wasn't a killer dog that did it. It was a human. Not that I mind humans slaughtering each other. I mean, it's what they do. But they shouldn't slaughter my human."

"I guess," I said dubiously. I didn't agree with him, though. All the humans I knew were pretty great, and they would definitely not slaughter other humans. But I guess I could see where he was coming from.

"You know, I don't even want to know. It's all so very troubling."

"But you can confirm that the killer was a masked intruder, right?"

"Yeah. A masked intruder with a big meat cleaver. And now can you please just leave me alone so I can properly wallow in my misery? This is quickly turning into the worst day of my entire life."

"All right, Kane," I said, walking over and patting him on the back, being careful not to use my claws. "I'm sorry for your loss, buddy."

"Yeah, yeah. Save it for the funeral. Oh, and when you see that deranged friend of yours? Tell him that if he ever comes near me again..." He hesitated, thinking hard. Then his face cleared. "Tell him I'll sic my killer dog friend with the jaws of steel on him, and he'll devour him in one chomp."

Dooley was surprised. "I thought you said the killer dog didn't exist?"

Kane grinned. "Well, he doesn't know that, does he?"

Which just goes to show even dogs have a measure of intelligence.

Dooley and I stalked off, leaving Kane to feel sorry for himself.

"I kinda dig that dog," said Dooley. "He's goofy but nice."

"Yeah, he's all right, as dogs go," I said noncommittally.

"A little sad, though."

"Which is to be expected. If Odelia were killed I'd be sad, too."

"You'd still have me and Harriet and Marge and Gran and Dr. Poole."

"True, but Kane has the rest of the Kenspeckles and he's still sad."

Kane had Shayonne, Shalonda, Shantel, Sandy, Steel, Camille and Starr Kenspeckle to take care of him. Obviously they were no match for Shana.

We wandered out of the kitchen and down the corridor to the suite of bedrooms. At the end, the corridor took a left turn, ending in an airy and light atrium, where a flight of stairs led down into a basement, and up to the second floor. Voices drifted up to us, so we decided to go and take a look.

"Hey, this might lead to the underground dungeon where the Kenspeckles keep their killer dog," said Dooley.

"We've established that, that dog is a figment of Brutus's imagination, Dooley."

"Oh. Right. I forgot. Still, it would be pretty cool if was real, huh?"

"I don't think so. A dog like that—if it did exist—would eat us for breakfast. Literally. And I don't know about you, but I value my life."

All nine of them, actually. We trotted down the stairs and

found ourselves in a pretty neat space. Several rooms led off a center hallway. The signs on the doors announced this was where we could find a bar, a game room, an office, a library, and even a nightclub.

"Hey, this is way cool," said Dooley.

"Yeah, like a playhouse for grownups."

As we neared the end, the voices became louder, and we saw that we'd arrived at the Spa & Wellness Center. The glass door was a little steamed up, and I pushed it open with my paw. We found ourselves in a darkened space, wall sconces casting a dim light, soft new age music providing a meditative atmosphere. Two men were face down on massage tables while two young ladies in white uniforms worked out the kinks in their shoulders and backs.

"Now this is what I'm talking about," I said. "This is the life."

"Being kneaded like a hunk of dough? We're cats, Max, not bread."

"It's a massage parlor," I said. "This is where they massage your muscles until they're smooth and flexible."

"My muscles are always smooth and flexible."

I glanced at the skinny ragamuffin. "That's because you don't have any."

"That's not possible, Max," he said. "Without muscles my skeleton would simply collapse."

I keep forgetting that Dooley also watches the Discovery Channel. And it seems that from time to time he even manages to pay attention.

We ambled over to take a closer look, and I saw that both men had their heads stuffed into some kind of leather donut attached to the table. But even though their faces looked all scrunched-up and funny, they still managed to keep up a conversation. I now recognized them as Dion Dread, Shayonne's husband, and Alejandro Salanova, the director of the Kenspeckles show. Neither man paid any attention to us, as usual. They were too busy talking.

"So it's a done deal, then?" asked Dion.

"I still have to run it by the network," said Alejandro.

"But that's just a formality, right? As long as the producer's on board, the network is bound to give us the go-ahead."

"Yeah, I think it's a cinch. We've never done a show like this before. What happens after you've been dumped by a Kenspeckle. It's bound to be a hit."

"I haven't been dumped," Dion protested. "Shayonne and I parted ways amicably. Irreconcilable differences and all of that stuff."

"You can't bullshit me, Dion. I was there when you had your big showdown with Shayonne, remember? Too bad the cameras weren't rolling, or we wouldn't have to reshoot those scenes. And at such a bad time, too."

"Great time, you mean. All the attention is going to be on us now, with Shana's body being found and the police sniffing around for the killer."

"Well, that's one way of looking at it, I guess."

"Always look for the silver lining, Alejandro. That's my motto." He tried to grin, but it was hard with his face squeezed into that funny-looking donut.

I shared a look with Dooley. So Dion was getting his own show. That wasn't going to sit well with the Kenspeckles. The only reason he'd risen to fame was because he'd married into the family. Now he was going to try and monetize that fame by establishing his own brand. I could see that this entire breakup with Shayonne and the murder of Shana was going to be benefiting him. If that wasn't enough motive for murder I didn't know what was.

"We have to tell Odelia," I told Dooley.

"Tell her what? That two guys are getting a massage in the basement?"

"That Dion is getting his own show. I'll bet it's a big secret."

"So? Getting his own show doesn't make him a murderer, does it?"

"It sure does. He could have set this all up to launch his new show."

Dooley gave me a worried look. "That sounds pretty far-fetched, Max."

"No more far-fetched than a giant killer dog biting people's heads off."

He laughed, and then I laughed, and then we both laughed up a storm. It's fun to laugh at a bully, at least when he's not around. Until he is.

"Laugh all you want, bozos," a gruff voice suddenly announced.

When we whirled around, we saw Brutus right behind us, looking pissed.

I gulped a little. "And? Any luck finding your vicious killer dog?"

Next to me, Dooley tried to suppress a giggle, but failed miserably.

Brutus fixed us with his best scowl. "I didn't find a killer dog, but I did just overhear a very interesting conversation. A conversation that will interest Odelia a lot."

"Hey. We heard it first," I said, alarmed.

"Yeah, and *we're* going to tell Odelia," Dooley added.

Brutus gave us an evil grin. "Not if I tell her first, you're not."

And then he slammed the door to the Spa & Wellness Center in our faces.

Chapter 12

The interview concluded, Odelia and Chase crossed the lawn back to the house. They'd briefly talked to the cameraman. His name was Burr Newberry and he'd been out partying all night. He met a nice girl in a beach bar and they'd spent the night together. Since Odelia happened to know the girl, she'd called her and she'd confirmed Burr's alibi. He was in the clear.

Shayonne and Shalonda had decided to go for a walk along the beach to clear their heads, though judging from the fact they'd asked Burr to tag along with his camera, not much head-clearing was going to get done. It made Odelia wonder if there was any part of the girls' lives that wasn't an act.

"I don't understand how people can live like that," she said.

"Like what?"

"Like this," she exclaimed, gesturing at the house and the grounds.

"In blatant luxury? I think it's pretty sweet," Chase said with a grin.

"You know what I mean. To live your whole life in the public eye."

"I'm sure those cameras aren't always rolling, and the sisters aren't always on. They're actors, and this is their show. Once the shoot is over, they go back to their regular lives. Driving their hundred-thousand-dollar cars, wearing their hundred-thousand-dollar dresses and sleeping on their hundred-thousand-dollar mattresses. You know, just like the rest of us."

"I still think it's weird."

"I actually think *you'd* be perfect for a reality show. You and your family."

"Me? We're pretty much the most boring family in the world."

"Oh, I don't think so. A reporter who just happens to be a sleuth? A mother who singlehandedly teaches Hampton Cove kids the love of reading? A doctor who's the best physician in town—and a great guy to boot. An ace police chief for an uncle. And a grandmother who's..." He grimaced. "Well, I'll admit she's a little out there."

"And don't forget Max, Dooley and Harriet. They'd be a big hit, too."

He stared down at her 'Crazy Cat Lady' shirt. "I bet they would."

"So what about you? The top detective allowing a small town to take advantage of his detecting talents? Now that's the kind of story that inspires."

"You know what? We should do a show together, Poole."

"Now there's an idea." A special of *Say Yes to the Dress*. She could be the bride and he could be the groom. A hot flush lit up her cheeks. Jiminy Christmas. What was wrong with her? "So who's next on your list?"

"I thought first we'd do Dion and Damien, then focus on the TV crew."

"We should also check into Robin Masters, Shana's ex-boyfriend."

"Yeah, I'll look into that."

They found Damien upstairs, in his recording studio. As many of Merl Berkenstein's clients were recording artists, they liked to have a studio on the premises in case they suddenly got inspired and decided to record a song. The studio occupied half of the second floor, a private movie theater the rest.

They took a seat at the mixing console while Damien, headphones perched on his head, was bleating into a sizable microphone inside the vocal booth. He was a shortish guy in his middle thirties, with a smoothly shaved head, a ginger goatee and his trademark sunglasses he could never be seen without. His voice, blasting through the speakers in the control room, sounded remarkably anemic without the background music giving it some oomph. He also sounded pretty pitchy. Nothing that Auto-Tune couldn't fix though.

"Is it just me or is he singing awfully out of tune?" asked Chase.

"It's not just you. Damien isn't exactly the world's most gifted vocalist."

"I'll say. My cat sings better than this guy." Damien squeaked some more and Chase shook his head. "Give me Garth Brooks any day over that clown."

She was surprised. "You're a country and western fan?"

"Yes, I am. At least those guys can sing. And write a decent song."

"Don't tell him that. Or the interview will be over before it's started."

He leaned in. "That's the beauty of being a cop. You can ask whatever the hell you want, and they have to answer, whether they like it or not."

He was right. As a reporter she was always treading a fine

line, especially with these big ego stars. Cops didn't have to worry about that. In fact it was probably good tactics to rattle a suspect's cage a little. Get them to confess.

"I'm starting to like this police stuff," she said. "It beats being a reporter."

"Oh? And why's that?"

"Well, I get to ask all the tough questions and I don't have to worry about the interviewee walking out on me or threatening with a defamation suit."

Chase grinned. "We'll make a cop out of you yet, Poole."

A sudden thrill of happiness shot through her. It actually felt pretty great to be partnered with Chase. They made a great team. Like Cagney and Lacey. Okay, so maybe they were more like Lady and the Tramp. She could imagine sharing a plate of spaghetti with Chase. Or some meatballs.

Damien had finished recording his new song, if that's what it was, and exited the soundproof booth. The door made a soft hissing sound as he did.

"Mind if we ask you a few questions, Mr. LeWood?" asked Chase.

"That was one of my best takes yet. Did you appreciate the exclusive?"

"Oh, yes, Damien," said Odelia. "That was... just great."

"The track's going to be on my next album. I'm dedicating it to Shana." He shook his head. "I thought I'd record a song for her while I'm still feeling the pain, you know. Throw all my agony into that one song. Make it count."

"I know exactly what you mean," she said blithely. No, she didn't.

"Fire away, detectives," said Damien, straddling the mixing console.

"Oh, but I'm not a detective," said Odelia.

"She's a consultant, which amounts to the same thing," Chase said.

Damien spread his arms. "Like I said, fire away. I'm an open book."

"Is it true you and Mrs. Kenspeckle were facing some marital issues?"

She saw what Chase meant by not having to tread lightly. As a reporter this type of question would have been on the publicist's list of taboo topics.

Damien nodded. "It's not a great secret Shana and I were seeing a marriage counselor. It was on season seven, and again on season nine. And front and center in the new season. You a fan of the show, Detective?"

"Can't say that I am," Chase confessed.

"Too bad. There's a lot you could pick up. As a cop, I mean. It's all about the human condition and the different ways living in close proximity with other human beings can affect you as a person. A fascinating experiment."

"I'm sure it is. So what about those marriage problems? We spoke to your sisters-in-law and they told us Shana was having an affair with Dion Dread?"

Damien's lips tightened. "That scumbag. Bagging one Kenspeckle wasn't enough for him, he had to bag two. But we were getting over that. She was finished with Dion, and we were working hard to resolve our issues." He played with his wedding ring, an ornate gold band with a gigantic rock. "We were fighting for our marriage, and I can tell you that we were winning."

"What about you, Mr. LeWood? Any affairs we should know about?"

There was a flash of anger in the singer's eyes, but it quickly disappeared. "I can assure you there are no skeletons in my closet. I was devoted to my wife and my marriage. I'm a family man, and I was dying to start a family."

"Can you think of anyone who would hurt your wife?" asked Odelia.

He shook his head. "Shana was the sweetest, loveliest person in the world. She was loved by everyone. I can't think of anyone who'd hurt her."

"She must have made some enemies over the years," said Chase. "People she rubbed the wrong way. You don't get to her level of success without stepping on a few toes along the way."

The singer fixed Chase with an intent look. "There will always be haters, Detective, but we were keeping them far away from us. It's important to keep negativity at bay. To focus on the positive. We shielded ourselves from all of that negative energy and didn't allow it inside this bubble we'd created." He gestured around himself. "We created our own reality, and anyone who tried to tear us down was placed firmly outside of the bubble. It's a simple matter of choice. And we chose life and happiness. That's all I can say about that."

He had a lot more to say, but nothing that shed any light on the murder of his wife. When Damien offered to play his song again, so they 'could look deeply into his soul, and find the purity within,' they kindly declined.

The interview over, Odelia's impression was that Damien LeWood was a nutcase. Still, he didn't seem dangerous, and she couldn't imagine him killing his wife. He might be a little weird, but he came across as a devoted husband.

As she and Chase descended the stairs, he said, "Oh, I got a text from the coroner. Turns out we were right. The killer did drug everyone in the house."

"So both sisters, Dion, Damien…"

"And Shana. The film crew was fine."

She thought about this. It provided all the Kenspeckles with an alibi. Unless… "The killer could have drugged himself, then disposed of the chloroform in the morning."

"Good thinking, Poole. You're right. This doesn't mean anything."

They'd arrived on the ground floor, and decided to check Dion's room, to see if he was holed up in there. He was next in line for an interview.

Very conveniently, all the rooms sported a hand-painted sign indicating whose room it was. The signs were all inspired by Disney movies. Shana and Damien were Cinderella and the Prince. Dion and Shayonne were Belle and the Beast from *Beauty and the Beast*, their faces nicely rendered by the artist.

"I wonder if they change these out every time someone rents this place," said Odelia, as she let her fingers trail across the sign. It had been enameled.

"I hope they do. I wouldn't want to sleep in a room with that on the door," Chase grunted, pointing at the portrait of Dion Dread as the Beast.

An image of her and Chase's faces superimposed over the portrait flashed before her eye. She'd be Belle, of course, and he'd be the Beast. Yum.

She made to knock, but Chase simply pushed open the door. "Another benefit of being a cop," he said. "You can just barge in and nobody minds."

Well, that remained to be seen.

"Hampton Cove PD," he announced. "We would like to ask you a few questions, Mr. Dread."

Dion Dread stood in the middle of the room, completely

naked, droplets of water clinging to his body. It was obvious he'd just stepped out of the shower. He didn't seem to mind being caught *au naturel*. "Oh, hi, detectives. Come on in. Excuse the state of undress. I'm a big fan of air-drying."

Chase's jaw tightened. It was obvious he wasn't a big fan of Dion. "What can you tell us about your affair with Shana Kenspeckle, Mr. Dread?"

Dion languidly reached over, picked up a towel from the bed and draped it around his waist. He was built like an athlete, with sculpted muscles and great abs. He also had enough tattoos to keep a tattoo artist on a retainer.

"That was all ancient history, Detective. Shana had decided to end the affair and come clean to her husband and her sister, which she recently did."

"And how did you feel about that?" asked Odelia.

Dion walked to the window and gazed out, looking thoughtful. "I wasn't happy about it, I can tell you that. I liked Shana. She was very sweet and sexy. Her sudden conscience issues placed me in a very awkward position."

"Did she confide in you before she came clean to her husband and sister?"

"No, she did not. One day we were an item, the next I was confronted by my wife and told she was getting a divorce. You can imagine how I felt."

"I can imagine you were furious," said Chase. "A divorce meant the end of your cushy life as a Kenspeckle."

Dion turned and smiled. Backlit by the sun, he looked like a Greek god. Before becoming a reality star, he'd been a swimmer, winning multiple Olympic medals. "Look, I won't lie to you, Detective. I was extremely upset. On the other hand, the whole affair led Shayonne and me to do a lot of soul-searching. After the first shock had worn off, she agreed with me that our marriage the last couple of months had been a sham. Shayonne had been, shall we say, sexually unavailable to me for a long time, due to some personal issues she was facing." He shrugged. "Hey, I'm a guy. I have a guy's needs. When I couldn't satisfy those needs with my wife, I went looking elsewhere."

Yeah, this guy was a real prince, Odelia thought.

"And your wife was okay with that?" asked Chase gruffly.

"No, she wasn't okay with it, but she understood. Coming out here was a blessing. We spent the last couple of nights taking long walks along the beach, and talked like we hadn't talked in a very long time. I like to think that we rediscovered the spark that had been extinguished through disuse."

"And how did Shana feel about you remaining a part of the family?"

"She was fine with it. Like I said, she was a very sweet person."

"Wasn't it uncomfortable for her? To see her former lover all the time?"

"Before we were lovers we were friends. So we went straight back to being friends. I loved Shana a lot. I would never harm her. Or kill her."

"Not even to save your marriage and your position in this family?"

But Dion wasn't to be goaded. He merely smiled enigmatically. "Not a chance. I'm a man at peace with myself and my past. I made a mistake. I owned up to it. I'm a man reborn, Detective. This whole affair has made me realize that I love my wife, and that I want to start a family with her."

Oh, great. Another family man.

"You don't seem very upset about the death of your mistress," said Chase.

"Oh, I am very upset. Don't let my calm demeanor fool you. Inside I'm a total wreck, Detective. I loved Shana to bits, in spite of the fact that she dumped me. She was a wonderful person and I will miss her. We all will."

Somehow the words didn't ring true to Odelia. The man was entirely too slick, and the whole thing felt like an act. But then what else was new with the Kenspeckles? This whole dreadful murder felt like an act. It wouldn't surprise her if Shana suddenly popped out of the closet and announced she wasn't dead after all. So when suddenly the closet did pop open, she yelped, fully expecting to see Shana's face. Instead, Max and Dooley came tumbling out, and along with them a black robe, a mask and a very large meat cleaver.

"The killer!" Max announced. "The killer is right behind us!"

Chapter 13

It's not much fun being locked up, especially if you're a cat. We don't like it. It makes us feel trapped, and there's no telling what we'll do when we feel trapped. In our case what we did was stare at the door, hoping Brutus was kidding and would come back to save us. When a minute had passed and there was still no sign of the big brute, I figured he hadn't been kidding. Of course, even if he did come back, there was no way he could open that door. Nature, in all its wisdom, hasn't outfitted us cats with opposable thumbs. Imagine what we could do if it had. For one thing, we could open this door. And for another, I could make a fist and punch Brutus in the whiskers.

"I think we're stuck," Dooley said, showing his firm grip on reality.

"I think you're right."

We glanced over our shoulders at the massage area. Dion and Alejandro were still face down, chatting up a storm, kneaded by the capable hands of the massage therapists. It looked like they were going to be here a while.

"Maybe Harriet will come to the rescue?" Dooley asked, expressing a hope beyond hope that our friend would switch allegiances again.

"I doubt it. And even if she did, she can't open this door by herself."

"I guess you're right."

"Cheer up, buddy. There has to be some way out of here."

"Or we can just wait," he said, languidly stretching out on the floor. "Sooner or later that door will open again. It's inevitable."

"And let Brutus share our hard-won secret with Odelia and take all the credit? No way."

This is not something I'm particularly proud of, but I admit I have a competitive spirit. I like to win, especially when competing against a bully like Brutus. Nobody is going to come into my town and my house and try and steal my human's affection in this treacherous way. No way. No how.

"Come on," I said. "Let's find the back door to this dump."

"Oh, what's the point?" asked Dooley, closing his eyes. "Maybe this is the universe's way of telling us we should take a nap."

I gave him a poke. It was my way of telling him to get a move on. "Get up, Dooley. We're getting out of here and we're getting out of here now."

He grumbled a little, but eventually managed to defy gravity and get up. "Do we always have to be the heroes? Can't we just be cats for a change?"

"No, we can't. Being a hero is the American way. Now let's go."

We wandered deeper into the spa center and passed several sauna cabins, just waiting for some crazy human to allow himself to be boiled alive. How they can stand that kind of torture I will never understand. Bodies aren't made to suffer those temperatures. The worst part? Humans like being boiled. It makes me think they're probably a lot less evolved than they claim.

We arrived at an indoor pool. It looked pretty cool. When I stuck my paw into the water I discovered that it was. Definitely too cool for me. Brrr.

"This water is freezing!" Dooley cried.

"Humans like it," I said. "I've seen it on TV. First they broil themselves in those torture cabins over there. Then they jump into this icy water. It's supposed to be good for their health. Sounds like fake science to me."

"I can't imagine how torturing yourself can be healthy."

"Humans think hamster wheels are healthy, buddy, though they call it treadmills."

We walked the length of the pool and arrived at the Jacuzzi. The water was gently bubbling, steam rising from the surface. This was yet another thing I didn't understand. How humans could spend hours soaking in hot water. And then they were surprised when their skin got all wrinkly.

We passed the resting area, which was located in an alcove, a skylight allowing sunlight to slant in and warm up the spa visitors. Loungers were spread out around a small fountain on the floor, and soft music played from the speakers. This was where humans, after all that torture, passed out.

"Hey, this looks like a great place for a nap," Dooley said, and jumped up onto one of the loungers.

"No way," I said. "We need to get out of here so we can tell Odelia about our discovery."

Next to the resting area was a small bar, where the guests could grab a drink. I trotted behind the counter, hoping to find the back door. What I found was a small storage room. Boxes were stashed up high, and when I looked around, I saw that the room doubled as the electrical room. I dashed inside. The electric switchboard was here, as well as a lot of pipes crossing this space. One set of pipes led up, and disappeared into the ceiling.

"Hey, Dooley," I called out. "I think I might have found a way out."

Dooley came trotting up reluctantly. "What?"

"Look," I said, gesturing at the concrete ceiling.

He looked up and yawned. "Nice pipes. So what?"

"So this is our way out," I said enthusiastically.

He stared at me, and then back to the pipes. "I think you're delusional, Max. How is this our way out? We can't squeeze into those pipes."

"No, but we can climb them. See how there's a hole in the concrete up there? I'm sure we can squeeze through."

"Squeeze through? And then what?"

"Then we'll be one floor up, and I'm sure there's a way out up there."

"And I'm sure we'll just get stuck up there."

"Where's your spirit of adventure?"

"Trying to keep me alive. I'm not suicidal, Max."

"Neither am I." I fixed him with a firm look. "Look, Dooley. While we're dragging our feet, Brutus is sweet-talking Odelia into appointing him her new first feline detective, supplanting us in the process."

"Planting what?"

"I mean, taking our place in her heart, her home, and her life."

Dooley thought about this for a moment. "I don't think I like that, Max."

"Me neither. So are you going to give this a try or not?"

He stared up again, and sighed. "I suppose so."

Lucky for us, the pipes weren't those plastic slippery ones. Even with claws it's hard to get a grip on that kind of surface. I usually simply dig my claws in deep, but we had no way of knowing what was running through these pipes. If it was gas or water we might be royally screwed. Fortunately the pipes were covered with some kind of Styrofoam and were easy to scale.

I went first, clawing my way up, leaving a trail of styrofoam particles raining down. It was a lot easier than I thought, and soon I reached the ceiling and squeezed myself through a hole in the concrete. Now I was on the first floor. I was right: the pipes extended up, to the second floor and beyond.

"This is some real Indiana Jones shit, buddy!" I cried enthusiastically.

"Or one of those suicide missions," he lamented. "Like *Star Wars Rogue One*. The heroes save the universe and as a reward they get to die at the end."

"Oh, Dooley," I muttered. I think if Indiana Jones had had a sidekick like Dooley, he might never have gotten his hands on that Ark of the Covenant.

"We're going to get stuck up here. We're going to get stuck and we're going to die. Archeologists are going to find our mummified corpses a thousand years from now, wondering what the hell we were thinking!"

"We were thinking about our obligation toward Odelia. And for your information, we're not going to get stuck."

"How do you know?"

"Because I can already see the light at the end of the tunnel."

"Don't go into the light, Max!"

"Why not?"

"Because it means you're dead."

"I'm not dead. I can see light coming from somewhere ahead of me."

"That's what they all say, and then they're dead."

"Look, we've got nine lives, right? So have a little faith, buddy."

"That whole nine lives thing is just an old wives' tale, Max. I hate to break it to you but when we die, that's it. We're not coming back for round two."

"Can you just... shut up already? You're not helping."

"I'm the voice of reason."

"More like the voice of doom."

We were in some kind of crawl space between the floors. It was pretty dusty and stuffy in here, but I didn't mind. I did see light, and I decided to follow it, whatever Dooley said. It led to a small rectangular opening covered with a plastic screen. I gave the screen a nudge and it dropped down into the space beyond. I squeezed my way through and found myself in another dark space, a vertical strip of light directly in front of me. This was the light I'd seen. Not that I needed it. My eyesight is pretty good, thank you very much.

Dooley squeezed in right behind me, and bumped into my butt.

"Where are we?" he whispered.

"Why are you whispering?" I whispered back.

"Because I don't want to wake up the monster."

"What monster?"

"The monster in the closet."

Dooley was right. We were in a closet. Above us, shirts and blazers were hanging from clothes hangers, and on the floor, where we were, a suitcase was placed. So that narrow strip of light in front of us was... the closet door!

"We made it, Dooley!" I cried.

"Made it where?"

"Someone's closet, just like you said!"

"I didn't say anything about a closet."

Outside the closet door, I could hear voices, and I immediately recognized one of them. "Do you hear that?"

Dooley frowned. "Hey, that sounds like Odelia."

"That's because it is Odelia, and we're in a closet in someone's room."

I glanced around, trying to figure out whose closet this was. And that's when I saw it. Right behind Dooley. Chills ran up my feline spine.

"D-D-Dooley. Don't turn around, but the killer is right behind you!"

"What?!" Dooley cried, whirling around. He yelped in fear when he caught sight of the black-robed figure lurking behind him, a huge meat cleaver in his hands!

"It's the killer!" I cried. "We found the killer!"

"I was right!" Dooley whimpered. "We're going to die!"

We tumbled out of the closet, trying to get away as fast as we could. The killer jumped out right behind us, and the meat cleaver clattered to the floor.

I saw Odelia and screamed, "The killer! The killer is right behind us!"

I jumped into her arms, and so did Dooley, and that's when I saw it wasn't the killer who'd been inside that closet with us, but only his robe.

Odelia looked surprised, and so did Chase, who was also there. The one who was even more surprised, though, was Dion Dread. And as he stared at us, and at the black robe and the meat cleaver, he cried, "That's not mine!"

Yeah, right. That's what they all say.

Embarrassed, I jumped down from Odelia's arms. Indiana Jones would never jump into anyone's arms. Indiana Jones would face the danger head-on. And now that I'd discovered we'd been spooked by a robe, I was ready to do just that.

"Wait, what is Dion doing here?" asked Dooley. "Isn't he supposed to be down in the spa getting a massage?"

"I guess his massage ended."

"See, Max?" asked Dooley. "We should have just waited it out."

"If we hadn't climbed that pipe we wouldn't have found the killer!"

"It isn't a killer. It's just an old robe and a cleaver."

"Duh. That's the murder weapon, Dooley, and the killer's bloody robe."

Dooley yelped, only now understanding we'd caught the killer, and he was here in the room with us. We both stared at Dion, the brutal murderer.

Just then, Brutus came barging through the door, a little winded, and cried, "Odelia! Dion Dread is planning his own reality show!" He caught sight of us, and his eyes went wide. "Oh, shoot."

Chase took one look at the cleaver and the black robe, still crusted with blood, and his jaw clenched. He stepped up to Dion Dread, flicked a pair of handcuffs from his belt, and announced, "Dion Dread. You're under arrest for the murder of Shana Kenspeckle."

"But I didn't do it! That stuff ain't mine! Someone planted it there!"

"You have the right to remain silent," Chase grunted, and marched Dion out of the room.

"Hey! I can't go out there in just my towel!"

"Anything you say may be used against you in a court of law."

Harriet now came traipsing into the room. "What's with all the screaming?"

"We found the killer," I announced proudly.

"You certainly did," said Odelia, crouching down and giving me a rub.

Harriet frowned at her boyfriend. "Brutus? I've been looking all over for you. Where were you?"

He tried to look as innocently as he could. "Oh, just hanging out."

"He locked us up in the basement!" Dooley cried accusingly.

"Yeah, and he tried to give our scoop to Odelia," I added.

"Oh, Brutus," Harriet said, shaking her head. "I told you, this is not the way to win friends and influence people. This is the way to make enemies."

"They started first!" he said. "They're trying to cut me out."

"Nobody is trying to cut you out of anything, Brutus," said Odelia. She gave Dooley and me a stern look. "Look, it's really great that you guys managed to find the murder weapon and the murderer's robe, but you have to learn to get along with Brutus. I think it's high time you all became friends."

We stared at Brutus, and he stared back at us, defiant.

"I want you to shake paws and apologize," Odelia told me.

"Me? Apologize to him? What for?"

"Come on, Max. You know you haven't been very nice to Brutus."

"Me? Not nice to him? He's not being nice to me!"

"Look, I don't want to hear any more. You'll apologize and be friends from now on. And you, Brutus, I want to hear an apology from you as well. Max has told me about your behavior, and it's unacceptable. Is that clear?"

Now that was more like it. Brutus looked like he was about to refuse, but Harriet placed her paw on his back and he finally relented, hanging his head. "Oh, all right. I'm sorry, Max, for the way I've behaved. It was wrong of me."

"And I'm sorry for the way I've behaved," I said when Odelia cut her eyes to me and gave me a warning look. "I should have been much nicer to you."

We reluctantly walked up to each other and slapped our paws together.

"Now tell him you'll be friends, Max," said Odelia.

"Friends?" I asked.

Brutus nodded. "Friends."

Just then, Chase stuck his head through the door. "We have to lock up this room. This is now a crime scene." He stared down at the gathering of cats, and shook his head. "Your cats caught the killer, Poole. Amazing."

She smiled. "Yeah, that is pretty amazing. And your cat helped, too."

Chase quirked an eyebrow at Brutus. "So he did. Good work, buddy."

He walked out, Odelia in his wake, and Brutus, Dooley, Harriet and me right behind her. He then locked the door and pocketed the key.

"I'm so glad we're all friends now," Harriet said. "This is so nice."

I caught Brutus's eye, and the look he gave me was far from friendly. His next words confirmed this. "This isn't over, Max. You're going down."

"Not if you're going down first," I replied, a little lamely.

"Friends, you guys!" Harriet said. "We're all friends now!"

Brutus shrugged and displayed a nasty grin. "We'll see about that."

Chapter 14

"So? Cracked the case, huh, Chase?" asked Uncle Alec. He took another sizable helping of spaghetti, and ladled some more tomato sauce on top.

It was Thursday night at the Pooles, and as usual Alec had put his feet under the dinner table, along with his temporary roomie Chase. There was spaghetti bolognese on the menu, so Odelia got to relive the famous spaghetti scene from *Lady and the Tramp* after all, though she and Chase didn't slurp from the same plate. But then she wasn't a lady, and Chase wasn't a tramp.

She twirled the pasta around the tines of her fork and thought about the case. She had her qualms about Dion as a killer. How convenient that the murder weapon would be lying around in his closet. Too convenient. Why hadn't the uniformed officers found it when they searched his room?

"Yeah, that was quick work," Chase said, pressing a napkin to his lips.

"Is it true that the cats actually solved the case?" asked Dad.

"It's true. The cats are the real heroes here," Chase confirmed.

Dad shook his head and chuckled. "Unbelievable. Those cats have saved the day so many times now they should be made honorary police officers."

He gave Odelia a wink and she grinned. Her dad was Hampton Cove's resident doctor. He had his doctor's office right across the street from the Hampton Cove Gazette. He was a jovial fifty-something physician with a shock of white hair. He was also one of the only people who knew that his mother-in-law, his wife and his daughter could communicate with felines.

"Yeah, we should probably give them a medal," Uncle Alec agreed. He sat back in his chair and patted his sizable paunch. He was a large man, and a well-respected chief of police. He'd finally returned from his fishing trip, only to discover he shouldn't have bothered, as the killer was in jail. "The mayor was very happy," he said. "He was practically on the phone with the FBI when you arrested Dion Dread. Good thing you nabbed him when you did."

"It still remains to be seen if we've got the right guy," said Chase. "But all the evidence so far points in his direction."

"Oh, don't be so modest, Chase," said Mom. "You nailed the perp."

Mom had been reading Lincoln Rhyme novels. The lingo rubbed off.

"Thank you, ma'am. I mean, Marge," said Chase.

He seemed more relaxed now that the killer was behind bars.

"I just knew that Dion was the perp," said Gran. The wizened old lady was polishing off her second plate of pasta. She claimed she was on the paleo diet, but Odelia doubted cavemen had ever been into spaghetti bolognese.

"Why is that?" asked Odelia. Gran watched the Kenspeckles religiously.

"Oh, I hate the guy. Even when he was an Olympic swimmer. That man's got more tattoos than Ed Sheeran. He's like a walking adult coloring book."

"I take it you're not a fan of the Kenspeckles?" asked Chase.

"Of course I'm a fan. I'm a big fan of the Kenspeckles. I'm their number one fan. Where else are you gonna find that much drama? It's better than *General Hospital.* And why is that? Because the Kenspeckles are the real deal. They're not something some Hollywood screenwriter with spectacles, pimples and stinky ramen noodle breath cooked up. It's all real."

"Except for Shayonne Kenspeckle's boobs," said Mom. "Those can't be real. They're lumpy and square. Real boobs aren't lumpy and square."

"You're right about the boobs. You got me on the boobs. They *are* square. But apart from that, what you see is what you get. All real, all the time."

"Or Shalonda's butt. I'll bet she got herself some of those butt implants."

"I'll throw in Shalonda's butt. Butt and boobs? Fake. The rest? All real."

"And Shantel's lips. I'm guessing lip injections. Lots of lip injections."

"Butt, boobs, lips, check," said Gran. "And don't forget about the botox. They all got the botox. Even Steel Kenspeckle got the botox, and he's a guy."

"Steel Kenspeckle's the dad," I explained, for Chase's sake.

"I know," he said. "I read Wikipedia."

"And what about Camille's rhinoplasty?" asked Mom.

"Camille's the—"

"Mother. Yes, I know," said Chase.

"And then there's Starr's laser hair removal. The kid's got no hair left."

"Starr is the son," Gran said as an aside to Chase, who groaned.

"And don't tell me Shayonne's eyebrows are real. Those are microbladed."

Dad grinned. "I'm starting to think I got into the wrong profession."

"Yeah, Dad," said Odelia. "You should have gone into plastic surgery. There's money in plastic surgery. You could have been the Kenspeckles' personal plastic surgeon if you'd played your cards right. We could all be living in Beverly Hills right now, and I could be writing for the LA Times."

"It's not too late," said Gran, perking up. "I could use a nip and tuck."

No amount of nip and tuck could ever turn Gran into a babe, but Dad gracefully said, "You don't need surgery, Vesta. You're a natural beauty."

"I know I don't need surgery, but I could use a lift. At my age stuff starts sagging so much only heavy-duty scaffolding can keep it up. I'll bet if I had Camille Kenspeckle's surgeon he could strip off a decade. Can you believe that woman's as old as Cher and Dolly Parton? She looks like a teenager."

Odelia felt it was time to give her grandmother a reality check. "Nothing on that show is real, Gran. Everything is fake, and I'm not just talking about the boobs and the butts and the thighs and the noses. I'm talking about the fights and the dramas and the tantrums and the crying. It's all scripted."

"Nonsense. Nobody can fake all those feelz. Like when Shantel and Sandy were on vacay in Cabo and they got into this huge fight over who got to bag the cabana boy? You can't fake that kind of heartfelt emotion. We'll never know who did the cabana boy but I think it was Shantel. BCheeks cheated on her with the dog walker so she decided to get back at him."

Chase leaned in, and whispered, "I'm afraid to ask, but who's BCheeks?"

"Some rapper Shantel dated last year. A total tool."

He grinned. "I'm surprised you even know the name."

"Mom and Gran keep me in the loop."

"You really are into that show, aren't you, Mom?" asked Uncle Alec.

"I told you. It's nice to get a slice of real life for a change."

"What did you think of Shana Kenspeckle, Mrs. Poole?" asked Chase.

"She was a doll. Misguided, of course. Marrying that loser Damien LeWood was a dumb move. The guy is certifiable and should be locked up."

"She deserved better," Mom agreed. "That girl was a saint. An angel."

"She definitely deserved better than to be murdered by that asshat Dion Dread," Gran agreed. "The show won't be the same without her."

"Do you think they'll cancel the show?" asked Mom, eyes wide.

"They said they wouldn't," said Odelia. "Shayonne and Shalonda want to keep it going, and they seem to think this murder will give the show a boost."

"Yeah, but when all the hubbub dies down it's going to drop like a stone," said Gran, the self-professed Kenspeckle expert. "Those sisters can't hold a candle to Shana, and neither can Shantel or Sandy. And don't even get me started on Steel and Camille, or that moron Starr." She shook her head. "No, they've gone and killed the goose that laid the golden eggs."

"So they *are* going to cancel the show," said Mom with a sigh.

"No big loss there," said Chase. "I doubt a lot of people are going to shed a tear about the end of the Kenspeckles."

"I will," said Gran. "Now I'll have to go back to watching *Jeopardy*. I can only imagine how boring that's going to be after my weekly fix of real-life drama and wholesome family entertainment."

"I'm sure there are other shows," said Mom soothingly.

"Yeah, but none of them are as much fun as the Kenspeckles."

"There's Mama June and Honey Boo Boo," said Dad with a grin.

"Oh, please," said Gran. "I have my standards, Tex."

This elicited a snort from Chase. Gran cut her eyes to him.

"So when are you going to start dating Odelia, Chase?" she asked.

"Mother!" Mom cried.

"What? I'm just looking out for my only grandchild."

"I could do dinner," said Chase, nodding. "I could definitely do dinner."

"Oh, curb your enthusiasm," said Gran. "You two have a thing or two to learn from the Kenspeckles. When Shana and Damien met they hit the sack the minute they laid eyes on each other. Same thing with Shayonne and Dion. Or Shalonda. The woman's had more anaconda than any self-respecting ho."

"Mom! We have guests!"

Chase just sat grinning, and when he briefly locked eyes with Odelia, she thought she detected a mischievous glint. As if he wouldn't mind going all anaconda on her. The prospect made her knees go weak, while other parts of her anatomy tightened up considerably.

"So you've decided to stop pursuing Chase, Mom?" asked Chief Alec.

Gran waved a hand. "I'm all about family, honey. Odelia needs a man a lot more than I do, so I've decided to sacrifice my own needs for hers."

"That's very generous of you, Gran," said Odelia.

"Ugh. It's the least I can do. Before I die I'd like to dandle my great-grandchildren on my knee. Have a four generation picture in the Gazette. Is that too much to ask?"

"I think Odelia and Chase are old enough to decide for themselves, Vesta," said Dad. "Without anyone else interfering."

"And I think they need all the interfering they can get. It's obvious it's going to take them forever to bust a move, and I'm not getting any younger."

"I'll keep it in mind, Mrs. Poole," said Chase. He tipped back his root beer. Judging from the grin he gave Odelia he was enjoying the conversation.

"So have you found a place of your own yet, Chase?" asked Mom.

"Actually, I haven't."

"Still looking, huh?"

"Yep."

"You can always move in with Odelia," said Gran.

"Mom," said Mom warningly.

"Just throwing out a few suggestions. Take 'em or leave 'em."

Uncle Alec clapped Chase on the shoulder. "You can stay with me as long as you want, buddy. Heck, I enjoy the company."

"Thanks, Chief. But Marge is right. Sooner or later I'm going to have to find a place of my own."

"Well, if it's up to me it's later rather than sooner."

"Once the Kenspeckles return to LA, Merl Berkenstein's place will be up for rent," said Dad with a humorous glint in his eye.

Chase laughed, twin dimples creasing his cheeks. "Yeah, that'll happen."

"You could always get your own reality show," said Gran. "Just make sure there's lots and lots of sex. It's the sex that makes these shows so popular. That and the catfighting, of course. You got to have catfighting."

"Speaking of the Kenspeckles, here's to a successful solving of this case," said Chief Alec, raising his glass.

They all drank to the successful conclusion of the murder investigation, and Chase said, "To Odelia, whose clever pussy managed to solve the case."

He gave her a meaningful glance. Her pussy obviously intrigued him.

"So what happens now?" asked Mom.

"Now we process the evidence," said Uncle Alec. "The cleaver and the robe. Check them for DNA of the victim and, hopefully, the killer. And while we wait for the results, we interrogate Dread. Try to get a confession out of him."

"That'll be easier said than done," Chase grunted. "The guy insists he's innocent and that someone planted that cleaver and that robe in his room."

"Once we get his DNA on the robe he'll sing like a canary," said Alec.

Odelia wasn't so sure. "What if he's right and he didn't do it?"

"Then we're back to square one," said Chase. "Why? You think he's innocent?"

She chewed her lip. "Why would he keep the murder weapon in his closet for us to find? That just seems like a dumb move."

"But we *didn't* find it. At least not when we searched his room the first time. He probably hid it somewhere else, then when his room was cleared he moved it, waiting for us to leave so he could dispose of it permanently."

"Yeah, that's what I think happened, too," said Uncle Alec with a nod.

"He always was a dumbass," said Gran. "I'm glad he got caught."

"We're all glad he got caught," said Mom. "Who's ready for dessert?"

And while Mom brought out the key lime pie, Odelia figured

Chase was probably right. Dion had simply put the cleaver in his closet so he could get rid of it as soon as possible. And if Max and Dooley hadn't ended up tripping over it, he would have gotten away with murder. Which reminded her that Max and Dooley deserved a treat for the role they'd played. And Harriet and Brutus, too. She was glad the foursome were finally on the road to friendship. Especially Max and Brutus. She had a feeling they were going to be besties.

And then it was time for key lime pie. And more Kenspeckle gossip.

Chapter 15

The killer was caught so we could finally relax. That night, while the Pooles were sleeping peacefully, Dooley, Harriet and I snuck out. After all that hard work, it was time to have some fun. Odelia had given us some extra-special treats, and we were ready to sing our hearts out. You may think it's weird that cats would join a choir, but to be honest it's just an excuse to shoot the breeze. Hampton Cove Park is pretty quiet at night, which makes it perfect to do a little hunting, a little tittle-tattling and a little partying.

"Do you think Brutus will be nicer after Odelia's speech?" asked Dooley.

"I think Brutus will be super-nice," said Harriet. "We're all friends now."

She was in a great mood. The four of us being friends had been her dream all along, and now it was finally happening. I wasn't so confident that Brutus was my friend now. Especially after what he told me: you're going down. That didn't sound like something a friend would say. At least I didn't think so.

"It's so great we caught the killer," said Harriet, prancing gaily.

"It's so great *we* caught the killer," Dooley corrected her. "Max and I caught Dion, remember?"

"Yes, but Brutus helped, and since I'm his muse, I helped too."

It was the kind of convoluted logic I had a hard time understanding. Taken to its conclusion, you could argue that the whole world had helped catch the killer, while in fact Dooley and I had done all the hard work. Of course you could argue that if Brutus hadn't locked us up in the spa, we'd never have been forced to climb that pipe and end up in Dion Dread's closet. Honestly, with that kind of reasoning you could prove pretty much anything.

"And I'm so glad that you and Brutus are going to be besties!" she cried.

Dooley and I shared a glance and shook our heads. Yeah, right.

We'd walked around Odelia's house to the street and were now traipsing along, heading for the park. The moon was out and it was a beautiful night. One of those nights where humans like to bring out the barbecue set and the air is redolent with the smell of grilled meat, smoke and burned grease. Yum. But since it was way past midnight, the only scent I could pick up was ocean brine, the wind picking up a little. In spite of that, it was still warm out. The perfect night for cat choir. We crossed the street and found the park deserted, which was exactly the way we liked it. Humans tend to cramp our style.

"Brutus is such a great singer," said Harriet. "I'm so curious to see what songs he's got in line for us tonight. Don't you feel that since he took over from Shanille we've improved so much? He's a great conductor but an even greater coach. Sometimes I feel like he should be on *The Voice Cats*. He's got Adam Levine's focus and Blake Shelton's heart and sense of humor and he's really concerned about our musical development. I mean, he *cares* so much."

On and on she prattled. Dooley and I couldn't get a word in edgewise. Not that we tried to. When Harriet gushes about Brutus there's no stopping her.

We entered the park and made our way to the venue we'd selected for cat choir practice. It was a small clearing with a few benches, which we used to set up the different voice types. You had your sopranos, your altos, your tenors and your basses. Personally I'd always felt I was an alto, but Brutus had dumped me in with the basses. I didn't like it. They didn't have an interesting score. Harriet, of course, was a soprano, and always got to sing the solos. She was our very own Kiri Te Kanawa. The people who lived around the park got to enjoy our nocturnal concerts, too. Though they didn't seem to appreciate them all that much. At least judging from all the abuse they hurled at us. And the shoes. Everyone's a critic, I guess.

As we padded up to the clearing, I saw Shanille was already there, and so were about a dozen of the regulars, all gabbing away to their heart's content.

"Oh, there's Brutus," said Harriet, and she was about to streak forward when she noticed Brutus wasn't alone. He was chatting with a gorgeous Siamese and a very red, very fat old cat who sat chewing on something.

"Hey, isn't that Princess?" Dooley asked. "And look. There's George."

I nodded, transfixed. I liked Princess. In fact I liked her a lot. She was John Paul George's cat, the famous eighties pop singer who recently died at his Hamptons home. He'd lived there with his twelve cats, the oldest of which was George. The cats now lived with Johnny's boyfriend Jasper Pruce, who probably took even better care of them than Johnny had.

The fat cat caught sight of us and came waddling over, a big smile on his face. "Hey, you guys," he said. George must have watched too many Marlon Brando movies, because he sounded like the actor's character in *The Godfather*. "Princess told me you've got yourselves a genuine cat choir here, so I figured we might check you out. We already met your conductor. Brutus."

I nodded, still staring at Princess. The moon lit up her white fur, and she looked even more gorgeous than I remembered. God, she was pretty.

"Welcome to the show, George," Dooley said. "Are you going to join?"

"Nah. I have no singing talent whatsoever. Just thought I'd watch."

George was a British cat, who'd come over from the old country along with John Paul George, when the latter had tried to make a career in America. He was probably the oldest cat I'd ever met, but he still looked great. Probably all that grade A cat food Jasper fed his menagerie.

While George and Dooley got reacquainted, I trotted over to Princess.

"Hi, Max," she said in that sultry, smoky voice of hers.

"Hi, Princess," I breathed. I couldn't keep my eyes off her.

"You two know each other?" Brutus asked, sounding surprised.

"We met," said Princess, and gave me a bright smile that melted my heart.

"I was just telling Princess I might let her sing the solo tonight," Brutus said with a curious look in my direction.

"Oh, that's so wonderful of you, Brutus," said Princess. "I won't disappoint you. I sat by John Paul George's side for years, singing along. I like to think he drew inspiration from my presence. All artists need a muse, and I wouldn't be surprised if I was his."

I knew I was gawking, but I couldn't stop. I think I was drooling, too.

"A celebrity such as yourself deserves a spot in the limelight," said Brutus, nodding. "If you like we can work on your solos one on one. Do some private coaching. I don't like to brag, but I'm something of a musical prodigy myself."

"You would do that for me? That's so sweet of you, Brutus."

I heard a strangled sound and when I looked over my shoulder I saw that it was Harriet. She was staring at Brutus and Princess, making strange noises at the back of her throat. Either she was going to throw up, or throw a hissy fit and hit Brutus. Either way, she wasn't happy. And neither was I.

"I started cat choir to give struggling young artists such as yourself their first break," Brutus continued suavely. "Kind of like a mentorship."

"You didn't start cat choir," Harriet said. "Max started cat choir."

At the mention of my name, I snapped out of my stupor. She was right. Brutus was putting the moves on Princess, and I was letting him.

"Yeah, I started cat choir," I said. "Dooley and I did."

Princess turned a pair of cool blue eyes on me. "You started cat choir?"

"Yes, they did," said Harriet heatedly. "And what's more, *I'm* the choir's lead soprano. *I* have the best voice. *I* sing the solos. Not you. Me."

Princess fluttered her eyes over Harriet, apparently wasn't impressed, and dismissed her with a flick of her paw. "I'd be delighted to sing the lead."

"Didn't you hear what I just said?!" Harriet exclaimed. "Tell her, Brutus. Tell her I sing the solos."

"Now, now," said Brutus airily. "This is not the time for petty rivalries. We have to think of cat choir. What's good for cat choir is good for all of us. And what we need right now is to boost our reputation. Attract top talent. A celebrity like Princess adds luster to the lineup. And luster is what we want."

For a moment, I thought Harriet was going to do a Miss Piggy and smack Brutus in the face, but at the last moment she restrained herself, and simply lifted both her head and her tail high, gave Princess the dirtiest look I've ever seen, and stalked off. We'd entered some regular *Black Swan* territory now.

"Look, you don't get to decide who sings the solos," I told Brutus.

"Oh, yes, I do," he said, casting a worried look after Harriet.

I turned to Princess. "If anyone is the musical expert around here, it's me. Brutus may be the conductor, but I'm the beating heart of this choir. I'm the heart and soul of cat choir. So if anyone is going to be coaching you, it's me."

"Is that a fact?" asked Brutus.

"That is a fact," I said.

He narrowed his eyes at me, and raised an extended claw. The same claw he used to direct the choir. "You may have started this choir, buddy, but without me you'd still be a ragtag clowder of bumbling amateurs. It took a real leader like me to turn this hapless bunch of losers into a real choir."

"Oh, you certainly are a real leader, Brutus," Princess said. She placed her paw on his front leg and felt his bicep. "And you're so very strong."

I drew up closer and puffed out my chest. "You'll have to forgive Brutus, Princess. He's new in town. He doesn't know I started this choir to build a sense of community here in Hampton Cove. Forge bonds. Inspire friendship. That's what I do. I'm a community leader. A leader of the community."

"I can see that," said Princess. She let go of Brutus, draped her front leg through mine and squeezed my non-existent bicep. "I like you, Max."

I practically coughed up a hairball. "I like you, too," I squeaked.

"You're a regular musical prodigy," Princess said. "Sing something."

"Huh?"

"Sing something for me. Give me a sample of your talent."

I cast about helplessly for a moment, but when I caught Brutus grinning at me, I pulled myself together and sang the first thing that came to mind. "*Is it too late to say sorry?*" I bleated. Princess blinked. My singing sounded as if a cat had stepped on my tail. "*Cause... I'm missing more than just your... body.*"

Princess emitted a wild giggle, then controlled herself with some effort and shook her head. "That was... interesting. Very... novel."

Oh, God. I'd screwed up, hadn't I? Stage fright. It's a real killer.

"You know, I was actually at the Kenspeckle place today," said Brutus, turning his back on me and starting to lead Princess away.

Her eyes went wide. "The Kenspeckles? The reality stars?"

"Yep. Hanging with Damien LeWood. Jamming with my main man."

"You know Damien LeWood?" she asked excitedly. "The famous rapper?"

"The one and only. Damien and I are tight. If you like I'll introduce you."

"Ooh, Brutus. I would love that!"

I watched Brutus lead her to a nearby tree, explaining to her how his buddy Damien LeWood had promised him a leading role in his reality show, and how he was pretty sure he could get her a casting call with the director.

"Max, what's going on?" Dooley asked, looking worried. "Why were you singing that horrible song? I thought we said we wouldn't do that again."

"I was trying to impress Princess," I said miserably.

He looked at Princess. "She doesn't look impressed. At least not by you."

I groaned. "I know. It was a total fail. And now she's all over Brutus."

He shrugged. "So? What's it to you?"

I stared at him. "Are you blind? She's the prettiest cat for miles around."

"I always thought Harriet was the prettiest cat for miles around."

"Well, I don't. And if I don't figure out a way to trump Brutus I'll lose my chance."

"Why don't you climb a tree?" he suggested.

"Climb a tree? What do you mean, climb a tree?"

"I mean climb a tree. Chicks dig it. They clap and cheer. It's a thing."

It shows how far gone I was that I seriously contemplated Dooley's inane suggestion. He's my best friend, but he's also an idiot, and the fact that even before he finished telling me to climb a tree I was scooting up the nearest tree, proves that when it comes to women, I'm an even bigger idiot.

"Yoo-hoo, Princess!" I shouted when I'd reached the first branch. "Why don't you come up and join me? These are the best seats in the house!"

"Oh, Max," Princess laughed. "You're so funny!"

Funny wasn't what I was going for, but at least I had her attention.

Brutus scowled at me, and within seconds he'd joined me,

clawing his way up to the branch directly above mine. “My seat is even better!” he yelled. “In fact this is the conductor’s spot. Make sure everyone can see me.”

Princess laughed again, a breathy, coquettish sound. It was so sexy.

I decided I wasn’t going to be outdone by this brute, so I quickly clambered up one more branch, and then I was one up on Brutus.

From the ground, Dooley gave me two thumbs up. “Doing great, Max!”

The other cats all stared at us as if we’d lost our minds. Even George stood shaking his weary old head. For the first time I was starting to wonder if I wasn’t making an absolute fool of myself. Unfortunately, Brutus wasn’t making this consideration, as he quickly outdid me, and rose one more level.

“Brutus!” a voice rang out. “Come down at once!”

It was Harriet. Apparently she’d returned to butt heads with Princess once again. She wasn’t going to give up on Brutus without putting up a fight.

“Not a chance!” Brutus croaked. “I have a choir to conduct.”

“You never do your conducting from up there!” she shouted.

“Oh, yes, I do,” he said with a chuckle. “Don’t listen to her, Princess. She doesn’t know what she’s talking about.”

Harriet turned to Princess. “I do know what I’m talking about. I’m not just this choir’s leading lady and main vocalist, I’m also Brutus’s girlfriend.”

“Not anymore, you’re not,” Dooley muttered, and Harriet gave him a withering look that quickly shut him up.

As Princess and the others watched, Brutus and I climbed higher and higher into the tree. Each time he overtook me, I went higher, and on and on it went, until we both reached the top and there was no more tree left. Huh.

Unfortunately we were now so high up that we couldn't even see the ground, or the others. And as we listened to the sounds of cat choir starting their rehearsal without us, I wondered what the hell I was doing up here.

"Um, Brutus?" I asked, precariously perched on the top branch.

"Yeah?" he said a little uncertainly.

"Do you know how to get down from here?"

There was a momentary silence, then he confessed, "Nope."

We both looked down, and the dizzying height gave me the creeps.

"They've started without us," I said.

"I know. Can you believe it?"

"And Princess didn't join us."

"I think she lost interest about halfway through our climb."

"I like that cat."

"Me too. Though to be honest I like Harriet more."

"What?! Then why did you put the moves on Princess?"

He shrugged. "I'm a cat, Max. Putting the moves on felines is what I do."

We were quiet for a while, sitting there side by side while we listened to the cats singing up a storm. Then the first neighbor opened his window and shouted something. Then the second neighbor opened his window and threw a shoe. Sound carries, and the sound of two dozen cats screeching as if their whiskers are being plucked from their faces with tweezers carries even more. Not that I'm not proud of cat choir, but I may have exaggerated a little when I was telling Princess how good we are. Actually we kinda suck. Big time.

"How are we going to get out of this tree?" I asked.

"Beats me," Brutus said. "I've never climbed this high before."

He sounded just as unnerved as I was feeling.

"Max?" he asked.

"Uh-huh."

"If we get out of this alive, I want you to know I think you're pretty brave."

"Come again?"

"Discovering that murder weapon today? That took guts."

"I only climbed that pipe because you locked us up."

"You know why I did that, right?"

"Actually, I don't."

He hesitated. "The thing is... Chase isn't my human."

"He's not?" This surprised me. "But I thought—"

"His mother is. She took me in straight from the nest. But then she got sick and had to go and live in some place where cats are not allowed, so Chase had to decide whether to put me in a shelter or to keep me. Lucky for me he kept me, but... well, let's just say Chase isn't much of a cat person."

"No, he doesn't strike me as one."

"I mean, he never cuddles me, or scratches me behind my ears. He just feeds me and that's it."

"Yeah, but he feeds you real meat."

He gave me a sad glance. "I'd trade all that for a cuddle. You and Odelia? You guys have such a great bond. She cares about you, and even lets you sleep on the bed and all."

"Chase doesn't let you sleep on the bed?"

"Never. He kicks me out of the house when he goes to bed."

"That's not very nice."

He shrugged. "It's all he knows, I guess. His mother was the same. Cats aren't supposed to sleep in the house. They should be outside. Catch mice."

"It's nice to sleep on the bed," I said. "Nice and warm and soft.

In the morning I like to snuggle up to Odelia and she hugs me. Makes me feel all warm and fuzzy."

"I'd like that," he said softly. "I'd like to have a human who cares about me like that. That's why I wanted to be the one to tell her about Dion Dread's new show. That way she might want to, you know, adopt me, maybe?"

I hesitated, then said, "You know, if you like we can share Odelia. She's got a big enough heart for two."

He was silent for a beat, then said huskily, "Thank you, Max. I'd really like that."

"Then that's what we'll do. You practically live with us anyway, so..."

He glanced at me. "You're all right, Max."

"You're all right, too, Brutus."

We gave an awkward high five and then lapsed into silence once more. All this talk of Odelia was fine and dandy, but if nobody came to save us, we'd probably never see her again. I just hoped Dooley was calling 911.

Chapter 16

Odelia woke up from a pronounced whispering nearby. She'd been dreaming of Chase, more particularly Chase's remarkably soft lips, and she so didn't want to wake up right now. The whispering persisted, and she dragged her mind back from her sweet dreams to the cold reality of her empty bed. Well, not completely empty. Two cats were seated next to her in the darkness.

She moved, and the whispering stopped. She closed her eyes, ready for more Chase. The whispering started again, Dooley and Harriet having some kind of argument.

"God. What's with all the whispering?!"

"No, I'm not telling her," Harriet was saying.

"We have to tell her," Dooley said. "We can't just leave them up there."

"We can and we will," Harriet insisted stubbornly.

Odelia smacked her lips. The pressure of Chase's lips against hers lingered. If Real Chase was as good a kisser as Dream Chase she was hoping her dream might turn into a reality one day. Maybe the day hell froze over.

"Leave who where?" she finally asked, giving up on her dream.

"Max and Brutus are stuck in a tree," said Dooley.

"Dooley!" hissed Harriet. "I told you not to tell her!"

"Look, I don't care about Brutus, but this is Max we're talking about. He could be stuck up there for days! Or even forever!"

"Serves him right. Serves them both right. They shouldn't have made such a spectacle of themselves in the first place. And all over some dumb broad. She can't even sing!"

Dooley giggled. "Yeah, she sounded pretty awful. No way she was John Paul George's muse. She fooled us all."

"Not me. She didn't fool me. Not for one second."

"What's going on?" Odelia asked tiredly, propping herself up on her elbows. She stared into the darkness. All she could see were two pairs of cat's eyes staring back at her.

"Max and Brutus decided to impress Princess," Dooley said.

"The skankiest cat alive," said Harriet.

"Princess isn't skanky. She's just... not a great singer."

"She is skanky. A classy cat would never get two cats to fight over her."

"Well, anyway," said Dooley, "Max and Brutus decided to impress Princess so they climbed a tree."

"Who gave them that idea?" asked Odelia, rubbing her eyes.

"Dooley did," said Harriet. "This was all his idea. Yes, it was!"

"I just figured it would give Max an edge. It looked like Brutus was winning her over and Max was very upset so I told him to climb a tree."

"So Brutus and Max were going after the same cat?" asked Odelia.

"Yes, they were."

"But I thought you and Brutus were a thing, Harriet?"

"We were. And now we're not. If he likes that stupid Princess he's welcome to her."

"So it's official now?" asked Dooley. "You and Brutus are history?"

"Ancient history."

"I'm so sorry," he said, though he didn't sound sorry.

"I don't care," she said. "I don't mind being single again. I'm too young to be tied down. In fact Brutus did me a favor. A big one."

"So where are Max and Brutus now?" asked Odelia. She was starting to get the picture.

"Still in that tree," said Dooley. "They can't get down. It's too high."

She did a mental head slap. "I better call the fire department."

"Or you could leave them up there," said Harriet, returning to her favorite theme. "At least a couple of days. That should teach them a lesson."

"I can't, Harriet. Max is my cat. I can't leave him up there."

"Then just leave Brutus up there. I'm sure Chase won't mind."

Yep. Cats were more like humans than people thought. A woman scorned and all that. "I have to get a hold of Chase. Tell him his cat is stuck in a tree."

She swung her feet from between the sheets and found her slippers. She shuffled over to the window and opened the curtains. It was still completely dark out, though on the horizon she thought she could detect first light trying to hoist itself over the skyline. It was doing a pretty half-ass job of it, too.

"What time is it?" she asked with a yawn.

Dooley had joined her at the window. "Um, like, seven?"

"So how long have they been up there?"

"Since after midnight."

"Oh, those poor dears. They must be terrified."

"Especially since Max and Brutus hate each other," said Harriet.

"Yeah, it wouldn't surprise me if they've eaten each other by now," said Dooley. "Like in that Tom Hanks movie? When he was stuck on that island?"

"Tom Hanks didn't eat anybody in that movie," said Harriet.

"That's because he was all alone out there, with nobody to eat. But Max and Brutus have each other." He paused. "I wonder who'll eat who. My money's on Brutus. He's bigger and tougher."

"Max is bigger," said Harriet.

"Yeah, but that's all flab. Brutus is all muscle."

"Nobody is eating anybody," Odelia said.

"She's right," said Harriet, sounding worried now. "They've got bark. Wouldn't they eat bark before eating each other? They've got plenty of bark."

"Would you eat bark when you could gobble up a perfectly succulent cat like Max? I don't think so," said Dooley. He sighed. "I'm afraid the only thing you'll find up there are a skeleton and a cat that looks like Tom Hanks."

"Oh, no," Harriet cried, and streaked over to Odelia. "You have to save them! You have to go out there right now and save them!"

"Relax. A couple of hours stuck in a tree won't hurt them." She hoisted up her jeans and slipped a sweater over her head. "In fact it might do them some good. Those two have done nothing but fight." Maybe being cooped up together in the same treetop might knock some sense into them. Or not.

"Men are so stupid," said Harriet, now practically in tears.

"Not all men," said Dooley. "I wouldn't climb a tree to impress Princess."

"Bet you'd climb a tree to impress Harriet, though," Odelia said, dragging her fingers through her hair. She knew Dooley had always had a soft spot for Harriet. Maybe now was his chance to score.

Dooley scraped his paw across the floor. "Maybe."

"Oh, Dooley," said Harriet. "You would do that for me?"

He looked up, hope dawning. "Of course I would. In a heartbeat."

She pressed a paw to her heart. "I take back what I said about you being responsible for Brutus and Max's being stuck. You're a true friend, Dooley."

"Friend?" asked Dooley, sounding a little disappointed.

She nodded, a smile on her face. "One of my very best friends."

Odelia grinned and grabbed her phone from the nightstand. As she left the room and headed down the stairs she was already dialing 911.

She arrived at the park the same time Chase did. Firemen were extending a ladder from the fire truck to the top of the tree. In spite of the early hour, Hampton Covians were flocking to, snapping pictures with their smartphones. Which reminded her... She took out her own phone and snapped a few shots. "For the Gazette," she told Chase. And Facebook.

All around, cats were staring up at the tree, enjoying the show.

A fireman climbed the ladder and disappeared into the foliage. Max and Brutus had sure picked a great tree to climb. From where she stood she couldn't see the top, even though firefighters had hit the floodlights and bathed the park in an eerie light.

Chase gave her a nudge. "So your cat and my cat, huh? Sitting in a tree."

She rolled her eyes. "I don't think they're kissing, Chase."

"You might be surprised," he said with a shrug.

"They're both males, remember?"

He frowned. "Are you sure about that?"

"Yah. Pretty sure."

"I'll take your word for it. How did you find out about this anyway?"

"Um... One of the neighbors heard them screeching and called me."

He shook his head. "think they'd have more sense."

You'd think anyone would have more sense than to climb a tree to impress a girl. She got a sudden flash of Chase climbing a tree to impress her. He'd probably look like Alexander Skarsgård in that Tarzan movie.

He gave her an odd look. "Why are you staring at my shirt, Poole?"

She quickly looked away. The man was ripped. Even through his shirt she could see his bulging chest muscles. He was dressed in a white T-shirt, a black leather bomber jacket, and a pair of skinny jeans hugging narrow hips. "So... how's the investigation going? Any word from the coroner?"

"Nope. But we're expecting his report today."

"Can I come?"

He grinned. "Sure. You can come whenever you want, Poole."

She felt a blush creep up her cheeks and directed her eyes firmly at the tree. The fireman was descending the ladder, clutching two cats in his arms. They both looked pretty sheepish. Especially since the gaggle of cats was happy to comment. And they weren't yelling their support. The consensus was that Brutus and Max were a couple of show-offs and got exactly what they deserved. Yep. Cats were pretty much like people.

"They look okay," said Chase.

"Yeah, it could have been worse. They could have eaten each other."

He cocked an eyebrow. "Cannibalism? Really?"

She shrugged. "Max gets pretty peckish after midnight."

"I'd like to see him try. Brutus would slay him."

She was sure he would. Which was why she was so surprised to see the two cats clutching at each other for support. It seemed that those few hours spent up there had brought them both to their senses.

"Look at that," Chase said. "Two little buddies."

The fireman finally reached the ground, and handed both cats to Odelia. She took them eagerly and pressed them in her arms. They clung to her for dear life. All around her there were oohs and aahs, and a loud applause for the fireman who'd risked life and limb to pluck two dumb cats out of a tree.

"They were up in the highest branch," he said, taking off his helmet and scratching his scalp. "Hugging each other. It was the damnedest thing."

"I told you," said Chase. "They're buddies."

She tried to hand Brutus over to Chase. He refused to let go.

"Look at that, Poole. He likes you."

She gave Chase a frown. "You're not secretly a cat hater, are you?"

"Me? I love cats. Well, maybe not love them, but I don't hate them."

"Brutus is not Chase's cat," Max explained. "He belonged to Chase's mother, but she had to go live someplace where they don't like cats so he ended up with Chase. He never even hugs him, Odelia. He doesn't care."

"I'm all right," said Brutus. "Chase feeds me meat."

"Yeah, but you can't live on meat alone," said Max.

Chase laughed. "For a minute there I thought they were talking to you."

Her frown deepened. "How many times a day do you cuddle your cat?"

He looked at her as if she'd sprouted wings. "Cuddle my cat? Um..."

Her lips tightened. She hated cat haters. "Adopting a cat is accepting a sacred responsibility, Chase. Cats need to be loved and lavished with TLC."

He stared at her. "TLC. Okay. And what's that got to do with me?"

"Brutus spends more time at my place than yours. Which tells me you're not taking particularly good care of him."

"Me? Not taking care of him? I love the little bugger." He gingerly patted Brutus. "Besides, cats are solitary creatures. They don't need TLC."

She raised an eyebrow. Both cats were still clinging to her like crazy and weren't letting go. "Do they look like solitary creatures to you?"

"Yeah, but that's because they just went through this ordeal. I'm sure they'll be fine once you put them down. In fact it wouldn't surprise me if they went scooting up the nearest tree the moment you do."

She shook her head. "You have to start taking better care of your cat."

"Look, he's not even my cat, all right? He belongs to my mom. In fact I've never had a cat in my life. I had a goldfish once, but that didn't end well."

"Well, now that you have a cat, you better learn how to take care of him."

He gave her a goofy look. "Maybe you can teach me?"

She blinked. "Teach you?"

"Sure. You're crazy cat lady, right? Teach me what you know."

She handed Brutus to him and he held him up so he was dangling. Cat and human stared at each other, sizing each other up. Neither looked happy. "Oh, for Christ's sakes," she muttered, and showed him how to hold a cat, with his left arm providing support for Brutus's backside and his right hand holding him steady. "Now just caress him. Cats love to be stroked."

With his big hand he patted the cat's head, practically squishing him.

"Not like that. Gently."

He stroked along Brutus's head. The cat had one eye closed and looked like he was ready to escape. "Like this?"

"Yeah, that's better."

Brutus seemed surprised. He turned to her. "Gee, thanks, Odelia."

She gave him a wink. "We'll make a crazy cat man out of you yet, Detective."

He grimaced. "Anything to keep this little sucker from waking me up at five in the morning."

Her eyes went wide. "Five? I thought it was after seven."

He scooted up Brutus's butt and checked his watch. "Nope. Five thirty."

She gave Dooley a hard stare. He shrugged sheepishly. "I was worried about Max."

"Thanks, buddy," said Max.

"It's so funny," said Chase, still stroking Brutus's head. "It's as if they're talking."

"Of course they're talking. Cats are intelligent creatures. They talk."

"I'll be damned." Brutus had closed his eyes, and was softly purring. Chase gave her a look of surprise. "Do you hear that? I think he likes me."

She grinned. "Congratulations. That's the sound of a happy cat."

Yep. She'd turn this tough NYPD detective into a cat lover yet.

Chapter 17

After tossing and turning for half an hour, Odelia finally gave up trying to get back to sleep. She dragged herself out of bed for the second time that morning, and headed into the bathroom. The moment she caught sight of her face, she yelped. Gah! Was this what she'd looked like that morning in the park? She looked like a contestant on one of those survival shows. The ones where they have to eat bugs and wash themselves in a stream. She quickly did the shower and getting dressed thing and headed down for breakfast.

Max, Harriet and Dooley followed her. They were uncharacteristically quiet. Max was still recovering from his tree adventure. Harriet was in mourning over the end of her affair with Brutus. And Dooley looked like he was trying to come up with a way to win over Harriet. Now that Brutus was out of the picture he thought he had a shot. Poor, misguided creature.

"I have to run, you guys," she said after munching down on a piece of toast smothered with butter and jam. "Don't do anything I wouldn't do, all right? Like climb trees and get stuck. I'm looking at you, Max."

"Can we tag along?" Harriet asked. "I need something to distract me."

"Sure. You can help me write a killer article about Dion. And about Max's adventure." She gave him a wink. "You can give me the inside view."

"Please don't," Max groaned. "I feel like such a sucker for getting stuck."

"Cheer up. Cats don't read newspapers so they won't make fun of you."

"They don't read the paper but they look at the pictures. When they see me, clutching Brutus and that fireman, they'll never let me live it down."

"Well, it's news. So I have to write about it. If I don't, Dan will."

"Oh, all right," he grumbled. "I'll give you my exclusive story."

She poured the contents of her coffee pot into the stainless steel travel mug her mom had bought her for her birthday and headed out. She opened the door to her old Ford pickup and her feline brood hopped up onto the backseat and made themselves comfortable. She'd put their favorite blanket back there and always had a plastic bowl and a few pouches of cat food lying around in case they got hungry. She flung her purse on the passenger seat, placed her coffee mug on the dash, and peeled away from the curb.

First stop: the police station. Charging Dion was a formality, so it should be over pretty quick. Next stop: the Gazette. Make Dan a happy editor by finally writing the definitive article on the Shana Kenspeckle murder.

She parked in the designated spot in front of the police station and hopped out, the three cats right behind her. While they went in search of the latest tidbit from the gossip mill in town, she waltzed into the station house.

As usual, Dolores was at her desk in the vestibule, ready to welcome the latest complaints from the citizenry, ranging from parking tickets, lost wallets and kids playing ding dong dash. She gave Dolores a finger wave and sailed right on past the display case showcasing Uncle Alec's fishing trophies. She entered his office at the end of the hall without knocking, and saw that Chase was already seated in front of her uncle. Both men looked pretty despondent.

"Good morning," she said cheerily, and placed her coffee mug on the Chief's desk. "Someone die?" she asked when she didn't get a response.

Her uncle flung a report in her direction and she snatched it up. It was the coroner's report. She quickly flipped through it, until she reached the section about the murder weapon. There was a lot of text and medical jargon and her eyes glazed over. "Just give me the short version."

"Dion Dread didn't do it," her uncle said.

Her jaw dropped. She looked at Chase but he nodded somberly.

"No way," she finally managed.

"Way," her uncle rasped. "Abe studied the wound and said he'd never seen anything like it, except maybe at the butcher shop. He said that whoever killed Shana chopped off her head in a single stroke. Which leads him to believe that the killer most likely works in the meat industry."

"Or the Mafia," Chase muttered.

"So? Maybe Dion Dread used to temp at a butcher shop?"

"I checked. He didn't. What's worse, Abe is convinced the killer is right-handed." He eyed her intently. "Dion is a southpaw."

"Maybe he switched hands? To throw us off the scent?"

Her uncle shook his head. "According to Abe that's an impossibility. The blow was administered with such precision and skill that there's no question. The killer was right-handed, and he or she knew what they were doing. Which rules out Mr. Dread. I cut him loose half an hour ago." He placed his hands on the desk, palms down. "I'm afraid you're up to bat again, team. Shana Kenspeckle's killer is still out there. Maybe planning his next kill."

Chase gave a shake of the head. "Always the optimist, aren't you, Chief?"

The chief shrugged. "Just facing the facts, buddy."

Chase cut his eyes to Odelia. "Ready for another day at the Kenspeckles, Poole?"

She nodded automatically. "Well, heck. I really thought we had our guy."

"Well, we didn't, so he's off the hook."

"Can't you arrest him for something else?"

Uncle Alec grinned. "Cheating on your wife is not a punishable offense, Odelia. At least not in this country. And neither is being a conceited ass."

Chase got up. "We'll interview the film crew. They might know something. Besides." He gestured to the window. "It's a beautiful day. Who doesn't want to spend it with America's first family?"

She groaned, and Uncle Alec gave her a commiserating look. "Better get moving, honey. Camille Kenspeckle is on her way over here. She's convinced it's terrorists that killed her daughter, and she wants the FBI involved."

She nodded and got to her feet. "We'll solve this case," she said, trying to project more confidence than she was feeling right then.

"By the way, how is Max?" Uncle Alec asked. "Not too traumatized after that tree incident this morning?" He had a twinkle in his eye. Her uncle was one of the few people who knew all Poole women could talk to their cats.

"Max is fine," she said. "A little shaken but fine."

"Brutus is fine, too, Chief," said Chase. "Thanks for asking."

The Chief leaned back in his chair. "Oh, but I know Brutus is fine. That cat is built like a tank. It's Max I'm worried about. He's such a snowflake."

"Ha ha ha," she said, and followed Chase out of the office.

"You know, Brutus has been purring up a storm all morning," Chase said as they walked down the hall. "I've been doing what you told me to and I've never seen him so happy. Who knew cats could be so clingy?"

"Yeah, well, cats are like humans, Chase. They need a lot of affection."

They reached the front door and he opened it for her, placing his hand on the small of her back. She cocked an eyebrow. "What do you think you're doing?"

He gave her an innocent look. "What you taught me. Giving affection?"

"I'm not a feline, Chase."

"You still need affection."

"Not from you, I don't."

He grinned. "Look who's being catty."

Chapter 18

The three of us were strolling along Main Street and I have to confess I was feeling out of sorts. This whole tree experience had rattled me. Until this morning Brutus and I had been sworn enemies, but up there, locked away from the world, we'd developed some kind of bond. The same thing happens to people shipwrecked on some desert island. I think it's called Stockholm syndrome. Though as far as I know Stockholm isn't an island. Oh, well.

We arrived at Wilbur Vickery's store, and took a seat on the pavement right outside, where Wilbur keeps his fruit and veg display. The General Store attracts a lot of cats, and Wilbur's cat Kingman is a real chatty tabby. So it's a great place to find out what's going on in town. I have to admit my heart wasn't in it today, and neither were Dooley's or Harriet's for that matter.

We'd just found ourselves a great spot in the shade, when Brutus ambled up. I looked at him. He looked at me. We looked away. This was awkward.

"So, what are you guys doing here?" he asked.

"Just hanging out," I said. "Collecting some gossip for Odelia's articles."

He shook his head. "You know? The weirdest thing happened this morning."

"I know. I was there, remember?"

"No, after that. Chase began to pet me and he hasn't stopped. Picking me up all the time, tickling my chin, fluffing up my ears. He even put me on his lap while he was doing research on the computer... about cat grooming! Says he's going to buy a brush and start working on my coat. Can you believe it?"

"I thought that's what you wanted?" I asked. "More TLC?"

"I did, but now I'm wondering if it isn't too much of a good thing. I mean, I'm not used to this, let me tell you. It kinda freaks me out, to be honest."

"You can't have too much cuddling," Dooley said, giving Brutus a frown.

"At least Chase is acknowledging you," Harriet said frostily.

Brutus gave her a sheepish look. "Yeah, Harriet, I, um, I'm sorry about last night, all right? I acted like a complete and total jerk. I don't know what came over me but I guess I was under the spell of that female or something."

Harriet stuck her nose in the air and snapped, "You *were* a jerk."

"I know," he said contritely. "And I'm sorry." He gave Dooley a glare when the latter started humming the Justin Bieber song. "Look, you know you're the only one for me, sugar plum. There's no one I love more."

Harriet's nose rose a little higher still. "You really hurt me, Brutus."

"I know, I know. And I'll make it up to you. What about I take you out to dinner tonight? I know this great little place where they serve the best veal in town. And there will be music, too. They've got a fantastic live band."

Her curiosity was piqued. “The best veal in town? And a live band?”

“Sure. The owner’s cat owes me. I removed a splinter from his butt once, but that’s not important. It’s called The Hungry Pipe, near the marina. We can enjoy a nice private dinner on the roof, and listen to that band swinging up a storm in the garden below. Best seats in the house. You’ll love it, babe.”

It was obvious Harriet was melting. She still had her nose in the air, but her tail was vibrating, which in her case usually meant she was excited.

“What do you say, sweet pea? You and me? Back in the saddle?”

Harriet smiled and streaked over to Brutus, rubbing her tail against him. “Oh, Brutus, you always had a way with words. You’ve got four yesses from the jury. So what do we do in the meantime? Still a long time before tonight.”

“We’ve got the whole day to ourselves, honey pie. A whole day to get to know each other all over again, and forget all about that nasty Princess.”

“Go on,” she purred. “I’m liking what I hear so far.”

“We can canoodle under a park bench, chase some ducks...”

She giggled. “You had me at canoodle, boyfriend. Let’s go.”

“Hey, what about the investigation?” Dooley asked.

“What investigation?” Harriet said. “They caught the killer.”

“See you,” said Brutus, and the couple strode off, giggling and cooing.

Dooley and I stared after them, Dooley looking pretty dumbfounded.

“What just happened?” he asked.

“Brutus and Harriet made up.”

“But why? I was just about to make my move.”

"Can I let you in on a little secret, Dooley?"

He blinked and I thought he was going to cry. "I suppose so."

"Harriet doesn't feel that way about you, buddy. She never will."

"But she can learn to love me, can't she? Given enough time, she might..." His voice trailed off, and now he was snuffling.

"Cats like Harriet are tough babies, Dooley. And tough babies don't fall for sweet cats like you. They need a tough guy like Brutus."

"I'm a tough guy."

"No, you're not. You're a sweetheart, and some cats don't dig sweethearts. One day you'll find the right cat, but that cat won't be Harriet, I'm afraid."

"I'm afraid you might be right," he said in a choked voice.

I patted him on the back. "You'll get over it. Lots of cats in the world."

He sniffled some more. "So what did you and Brutus talk about up there?"

"Oh, you know. This and that."

He gave me a sad look. "So you two are friends now, huh? Besties?"

I laughed. "I don't know what we are, but I'm pretty sure we'll never be besties." I gave him a light shove. "You're my bestie, Dooley. You know that."

He nodded and licked his nose. "At least there's that."

"Oh, and by the way, thanks for saving me from that tree. If not for you I would probably still be up there."

"Serious question, Max. And I want you to be honest with me."

I frowned, prepared for Dooley's deepest thoughts. "Shoot."

"Were you ever tempted to take a bite out of Brutus?"

I stared at him. “What? Of course not. Why would I want to bite Brutus?”

“Let me rephrase that. Did he try to take a bite out of you?”

“Of course not! Brutus may be a lot of things but he’s not a cannibal.”

He nodded seriously. “Oh, I see. So you ate bark, then?”

“No, I didn’t eat bark. I was too nervous to eat. I was stuck in a tree.”

“How can you be too worried to eat? I’m never too worried to eat.”

That was true. Dooley loves to eat. Even now, when he was down over Harriet and Brutus getting back together, he was sniffing at an apple someone had dropped. And I’m pretty sure Dooley doesn’t even like apples.

Just then, a car skidded to a stop at the curb. The door opened and Odelia stepped out. “Hop in, you two. We’re going back to the Kenspeckles.”

Dooley and I did as we were told. I saw that Chase was behind the wheel.

“Is this really necessary?” the burly cop asked.

“Cats love to ride around in cars,” Odelia said, slamming the door shut.

“They do?” Chase put the car in gear. “I thought that was dogs.”

“Nope. Cats love cars. They like to stick their heads out the window and flap their tongues in the breeze.”

“Pretty sure that’s dogs.”

She cocked her head. “Look, who are you going to believe, Chase? Crazy cat lady or some stupid internet site?”

He shrugged. “If you say so. Buckle up, you guys. It’s Kenspeckle time.”

"Again?" I asked. "I thought we were through with that place."

"Dion Dread didn't do it," Odelia said, and she did not look happy.

"So who did?" I asked.

She shrugged. "That's for us to find out."

Chase glanced over. "Are you talking to your cats now? Is that what you're doing?"

"Uh-huh. I told you, Chase. They're intelligent creatures."

He shook his head. "You *are* a crazy cat lady, lady."

He didn't know the half of it.

Chapter 19

Odelia and Chase were back for round two, but it was obvious from the moment they arrived at the gate they weren't exactly welcome. And why would they be? Yesterday they'd arrested Dion Dread, kept him to cool his expensively shod heels for one night and then cut him loose. The word about Dion's treatment at the hands of the Hampton Cove police must have spread, and the Kenspeckles were closing ranks and protecting their own.

Security had been beefed up, and they had a hard time making it past the gate. Two burly guards held vicious-looking Doberman Pinschers on short leashes, anxious to sic them on anyone who gave them the side-eye.

Finally, Chase's beat-up pickup rumbled through the gate and up the driveway. He parked in front of the house. Another day in paradise.

"I have a feeling we're not as welcome as we were yesterday," Odelia said as she let Max and Dooley out of the car. At least nobody could prevent the two cats from snooping around. She just hoped there weren't any Dobermans around. Even if there were, Max and Dooley could take care of themselves. Plenty of trees on the property.

"Yeah, I think they want this investigation over with," Chase said as they circled the house and headed to the back.

They found Shayonne and Shalonda by the pool, Shayonne engrossed in Star Magazine and Shalonda in Us Weekly. They both had cotton balls between their toes. They were reading with sunglasses perched on their rhinoplastic noses, their surgically enhanced boobs practically popping from tiny bikini tops. They didn't even look up when they passed.

Chase had set up interviews with the crew, and they headed for the guest house, which sat fifty yards from the main house. It was a backyard bungalow. Slate gray weatherboard with a nice porch. Big enough for a small family. Or a television crew.

On a concrete slab next to the house, a makeshift outdoor gym was constructed, and Stanbury Boa was on his back on a power bench, lifting a massive barbell. The veins in his neck stood out like cords as he bench-pressed the iron, his arms pumping up and down like pistons. He had a smoothly shaved head and wore a red bandana, a pair of American flag swim trunks and a lot of attitude.

"Hi there," Odelia said pleasantly. "Can we ask you a few questions? Is now a convenient time for you, Mr. Boa?"

He merely growled something and continued pushing out his reps.

Chase stepped up. "Hampton Cove police, buddy. Where were you the night Shana Kenspeckle was murdered?"

Boa racked the barbell and sat up, dusting chalk from his hands. "I was right here, guarding the property," he growled, hitting them with his best glare, the one he probably hoped would land him a role next to Vin Diesel in the next *Fast & Furious* movie.

"If you were so busy guarding the property how come you didn't catch the killer?" asked Chase.

The bodyguard's eyes darkened. He seemed foreign born, judging from his accent. "I was guarding the property against outside intruders. How was I to know that one of them—" He gestured to the main house, where Dion had just walked out and stood stretching. "—would kill one of their own?"

"So you think one of the Kenspeckles killed Shana?" asked Odelia.

"No one came onto the property. At night security around this place is tight. I see to that."

"Have you heard any rumors who might have done it?" asked Chase.

"I've heard no such rumors. But you may want to interview the sisters. They hated Shana's guts."

"And why was that?"

He shifted his massive shoulder in a shrug. "Sibling rivalry. They couldn't stand that Shana was more successful than they were. More popular."

"What about the crew?" asked Chase.

"You should talk to Alejandro," said the giant. "He would do anything to get his show to the top of the ratings again. Last week I heard him tell Burr that he was praying for a murder."

"He said that?" asked Odelia.

"Yes, he did. He said only a juicy murder would get people to watch the show again. They were on the verge of being canceled." He nodded curtly. "I think that's enough motive for murder, don't you, Detective?"

With these words, he lay back down and picked up the huge barbell again. With an animal-like grunt, he launched into another grueling set.

"Wow, I wouldn't like to get into a fight with that guy," Odelia said as she tripped after Chase. She had to take two strides for every one of his.

"Pfft. He's all show. I'll bet those muscles aren't even real."

"They looked pretty real to me."

"Trust me. It's all steroids, growth hormone and synthol injections."

Sounded like someone was a little envious. Then again, Chase didn't have to be jealous of Boa the man mountain. The cop was built like a Hulk himself.

The guest house was tastefully decorated. Like the main house, white was the dominant color, the floors a warm mahogany in contrast. They'd stepped into the foyer and the man they'd come to see was comfortably seated on a white leather couch, reading a copy of Men's Fitness. Alejandro was wearing a yellow polo shirt and beige slacks and looked like a million bucks. When he got up to greet them, he did so with outstretched hands and a killer smile. He kissed them on the cheeks. Twice. Surprised, Chase touched the spot. Bet that hadn't happened to him when he interviewed gangbangers in the Bronx.

"Please, sit down," Alejandro said. "Make yourself at home."

They took a seat on the white leather couch, and Odelia saw that Alejandro seemed very eager to talk to them. He sat ramrod straight and eyed them brightly, a smile on his face. Before they could ask him a question, he announced, "I think you should look into the terrorism angle again."

"We already established that the note was a fake," said Chase.

"Yes, but have you considered that perhaps this terrorist simply wasn't well-versed in the Arabic language?" Alejandro asked, his brows arching. "Not all terrorists have a college degree, Detectives. One might even make an argument that most terrorists never had any schooling at all. It's well established that a lot of them are ordinary criminals who turned to terrorism because it pays better and lends them prestige and self-esteem.

Most of them are not even ideologically motivated. They're simply in it for the money."

He continued with wide gestures of his hands. "You have a terrorist who's not schooled, who decides the Kenspeckles would make an excellent target. He does his business and leaves that crudely written note, merely showing he doesn't have a thorough grasp of grammar, and voila. Case closed."

Chase shook his head. "I really don't think the terrorist angle is a viable one, Mr. Salanova. For one thing, security around the house was tight that night, and we've already established that the murder was an inside job."

"So? That simply means this house has been infiltrated by a terrorist."

"Do you really think a terrorist would target Shana and leave the others unharmed?" asked Odelia. "Wouldn't a real terrorist murder the entire family when he had the chance?"

This gave the flamboyant director pause. Then he brightened. "Perhaps he's planning to do the others at a later date? Like a staggered terror spree?"

Chase, obviously bored with the terrorist angle, asked, "Where were you between four and five the night Shana Kenspeckle was killed, Mr. Salanova?"

His eyes went wide. "Me? You suspect me?"

"Everyone's a suspect until we find the killer, sir. So where were you?"

"Right here, sleeping in my bed," said the director. "Mentally preparing myself for another day of making the best reality show on the planet."

"Isn't it true that the best reality show on the planet was losing steam?" Odelia asked.

The director brushed a stray lock of hair from his brow. "Pardon?"

"We were told you were so anxious to boost the dropping ratings of your show that you figured a nice, juicy murder might just do the trick."

He waved an airy hand. "I may have made such a comment, but it was only in jest. I merely wanted to convey the message that it would take a miracle to get our numbers back up to an acceptable level."

"So you admit that your show is in peril?" Odelia asked.

He smiled that bright smile of his. She wondered if it was veneers or implants. Either way, his choppers looked amazing. "Of course I do. And I hate it. This show is a passion project. It has put my name on the map."

"So you would do anything to salvage your show—even commit murder," Odelia stated, taking a leaf from Chase's book.

Alejandro draped his arms over the back of the couch and leaned back. "You do have a way with words, Detective."

"Oh, but I'm not a detective," she said. "I'm a consultant. And a reporter."

"I knew it. Your facility with the language is remarkable. Yes, I would do anything to extend the life of this show. But I would never kill a person to do so. Besides, without Shana Kenspeckle this show is doomed. She was my star, the biggest and brightest celebrity to step onto the stage. With her gone, the show won't last another season."

"What about the rest of the Kenspeckles?" asked Chase.

"Shana was the reason people watched this show. There isn't enough star power in the rest of the Kenspeckles to carry the weight of such a show. Oh, I'm sure it will go on for a while. People will be curious to see the episodes we're shooting right now. But soon they'll get bored with the shenanigans of Shayonne and Shalonda and the others and that will be the end of it."

So much for the murder giving the show a new lease on life. "Can you think of anyone who'd want the show to get canceled?" Odelia asked.

The director quickly checked around, then lowered his voice. "Eamonn was very vocal about wanting to leave the show. Unfortunately the poor boy signed an ironclad contract that basically ties him to this show in perpetuity."

Chase checked his notebook. "Eamonn Dot is one of the writers?"

"He is. And he hates this show with a vengeance. Unfortunately he signed the contract back when he was an absolute nobody, and the network likes his work so much they're keeping him around, even though he's expressed a wish to be removed from the production. He's already had to say no to several other projects he'd expressed an interest in, because he's tied to this show."

"What about you? Aren't you anxious to do something else?" Chase asked.

"Oh, but I can," said the director. "I never signed such a silly contract. I can walk away whenever I want." He placed his hand on his heart. "But I so love my Kenspeckles. They're a part of me now, and I don't want to let go."

Probably the fact that he got paid a nice packet didn't hurt either. They thanked the director, who seemed disappointed they didn't want to extend the interview, and went looking for Eamonn Dot, the troubled screenwriter.

They found him out on the terrace behind the guest house, where he was typing up a storm on his MacBook. He looked a little rattled when they approached him, but then writers usually are a high-strung bunch.

"Eamonn Dot? Police," Chase said, producing his badge. "We'd like to ask you a few questions about the Shana Kenspeckle murder."

"Of course, of course," he said, quickly closing his MacBook.

They drew up a couple of iron chairs, the claw feet scraping against the hardwood, and launched into the interview. Odelia was starting to get the hang of this thing. Being a cop was all about asking the right questions, and trying to get the suspect to reveal stuff they didn't necessarily want to reveal.

"Is it true you were dying to get out of this gig?" asked Chase.

The writer, a bespectacled skinny type with thinning hair and a lot of pimples, blinked nervously. "I—who told you that? I mean, not that it's true."

"Just answer the question."

"I, well..." He looked around anxiously. "Are you going to tell the network about this? Cause I may not be completely satisfied with this gig, but that doesn't mean I want to antagonize the network. Never antagonize the network, Detective. They're the ones with the power to blackball you."

"We're not going to tell the network," Odelia assured him.

He bit his lip. "All right. That's good. That's great." He picked up a packet of cigarettes and offered them one. They both declined. He lit one up and took an eager drag. "I, um, yeah. Yeah, I wasn't happy with this job. I am not happy with this job. In fact it's probably the worst job in the world. Well, maybe not. Sewer inspector or professional dog and cat food taster or armpit sniffer are up there with being a writer for the Kenspeckles. I, um..." He took another long drag from his cigarette. "Yeah, writing those horrible treatments, outlining those stupid scenes, having to endure that hammy acting..." He shook his head. "It's all very draining. Excruciatingly draining."

Odelia had the impression the writer was mistaking them for his shrink, as the flow of words was almost unstoppable.

"So you didn't like the show?" Chase asked, stating the obvious.

"No, I don't like the show. It's the worst show on television and I'm in it up to my eyeballs. Can you imagine how soul-sucking it is to write the kind of terrible drama that is required of me? For one thing, I have to keep abreast of all the gossip. I spend hours and hours reading gossip magazines. It's brutal."

Hey, this job didn't sound so bad. Who didn't love gossip magazines? And this guy was getting paid to do it? Cool. "So why don't you quit?" she asked.

His hand trembled. "I—I can't. There's an exclusivity clause in my contract. I signed back when I was an absolute nobody and now I'm stuck."

"So you decided that the only way to get the show canceled was to kill off one of the principals," Chase said, nodding.

"Yeah—wait, what? No! No, I—I would never do that. I... I'm not a killer, Detective. I—I can't stand the sight of blood. And gore. I don't even watch *The Walking Dead*. Zombies freak me out. And blood. It's the senseless violence. It gets to me." He took another, long drag. "You sure you don't..."

"No, thanks, I'm good," Chase said. "Where were you when Shana was killed, Mr. Dot?"

He gestured to a window that looked out onto the terrace. "Right here. In my room. I'm in the smallest room in the house. More like a broom cupboard. Harry Potter size." He grimaced. "It's the curse of the writer. But that doesn't mean I killed Shana. For one thing, I owe my career to this show. Once it's canceled, I can get any job I want. And it's made me a lot of money. A fixed income. Do you know how many writers would kill their mother to get on a show like this? Thousands. Not literally kill their mother. It's just a figure of speech. Most of my colleagues are out of work. I may hate my job, and it's one of the soul-suckiest jobs on the planet, but it's a job. I get paid."

"Do you have any idea who might be behind the murder?" asked Odelia.

The guy put out his cigarette with nervous jabs and nodded feverishly. "One of the girls here got a really bum deal. She was attacked by Shana."

Chase frowned. "Shana got physical with a crew member?"

He expelled a jittery laugh. "Not physical, Detective, but she did make her life a living hell. Don't tell her I told you, but I think you better have a word with Laurelle. Laurelle Merritt? She's the stylist. She..." He coughed. "She had the bright idea to make a sex tape. She showed the tape to Shana, hoping she would make her famous. All Shana did was show the tape to her sisters. They found the whole thing hilarious and started sending it around to their friends as a joke. Laurelle was shattered." He blinked. "Shana Kenspeckle was the original mean girl, Detectives. The Shana you see on the screen? That was my creation. The real Shana was not a very nice person."

Chapter 20

Dooley and I had settled down at our new favorite spot: on top of that nice leather couch in the Kenspeckle living room. From here we had a great view of all the goings-on at the house, and could report back to Odelia with any new developments.

"We have to tell Odelia to get a nice couch like this," Dooley said as he dug his claws into the leather. "I like it. It's got everything a cat needs."

"I like it too," I said. "Though I don't know what the Kenspeckles are going to say when they find out you're ruining the couch, Dooley."

"I'm not ruining it. I'm merely adding my personal touch."

Rich people usually don't have cats. They have dogs, and train them not to ruin the expensive furniture. You can't train cats not to sink their claws into the upholstery. Not that we're dumb or something. We just don't care.

"So have you solved the murder yet?" Dooley asked.

"Nope. But I bet it's a guy. Butchers are usually guys. And according to Abe we're dealing with a real butcher. As in a professional meat carver."

"So Dion or Damien? But Dion is innocent."

"What about Damien? Rappers are butchers. Butchers of taste."

All right. So I don't like rap music. Sue me.

We both watched as Damien paced the living room, deeply engrossed in thought. From time to time he muttered a few snatches of song, punching the air like a kickboxer, then shook his head and paced some more. He was obviously in the throes of the creative process.

Dooley turned to me. "I don't think it's Damien."

"I think you're right. A doofus like that can't be the killer."

Which left... Boa the bodyguard, Burr the cameraman, Alejandro the director, or the writer. Or any of the other bodyguards. Oh, boy. Sleuthing had never been so hard. "I'll bet it's Boa," I said. "He looks like a butcher."

"Oh, look," said Dooley. "Speak of the devil."

The big bodyguard came lumbering up, the ground practically quaking where he stepped. He was all sweaty and oily, his big muscles flexing and moving beneath his tan skin. Man, the guy was ripped.

"I wonder why they haven't fired him," I said. "I mean, Shana was killed on his watch. You'd think they'd get rid of him as soon as possible."

We watched as Shalonda waved the bodyguard over. He bent over her, placing his hands on either side of her head, and then... kissed her. And I mean really kissed her. Not a brotherly kiss or anything but a no-holds-barred French kiss from what I could tell. He rose up, a giggling Shalonda dangling from his neck, he staggered to the pool, and they both toppled in.

"I think I know why he wasn't fired," Dooley said.

The moment they resurfaced, there was more kissing, and

before we knew what happened, Boa dispensed with Shalonda's bathing suit and our world suddenly turned into an X-rated movie. The kind Odelia doesn't allow us to watch. We both stared at the scene, transfixed, our jaws dropping.

"Um. I think I see what you mean, Dooley," I said.

I wanted to avert my eyes but I couldn't. It was like watching a train wreck. You just can't look away no matter how wrong you know it is.

"Max?"

"Uh-huh?"

"What are they doing?"

"It's called sex, Dooley. It's what humans do when they make a baby."

"Oh. So they're making a baby?"

"Uh-huh."

"I thought they were trying to eat each other."

"No. I'm pretty sure they're making a baby."

"Oh, all right."

Five minutes later, they were through, and since they were both still alive, it was obvious I was right and Dooley wasn't. They'd made a Kenspeckle. Shayonne seemed less impressed with her sister's shenanigans than we were. She was sleeping, her mouth open, snoring softly. Not a pretty sight.

Shalonda emerged from the pool and plunked down on her chaise. She looked exhausted. Apparently making new Kenspeckles was hard work.

I searched around for the cameraman, wondering if he caught all that baby making with his camera, but I didn't see him anywhere. Apparently making new Kenspeckles wasn't part of the setup. This wasn't Big Brother.

Just then, it was as if a bomb went off. Only it wasn't a

bomb but a leggy female with short raven hair and sunglasses covering half the acreage of her face. She strode up like a model on a catwalk, took one look at Shayonne, Shalonda and Boa, and bellowed, "Is this the way to greet your mother?"

Mother? And then I recognized her. Camille Kenspeckle had arrived. The original queen bee. She had a fur coat casually wrapped around her shoulders, and struck a pose, looking like the female version of Xander Cage.

Shayonne awoke with a start. When she caught sight of her mother, she squealed with delight, producing a sound so high only Dooley and I could hear it. And her sister, apparently, for Shalonda tumbled from the lounger, looked around dazedly, and scrambled up the moment she saw Camille. Both girls dashed around the pool and threw themselves into their mother's arms. Boa, who'd been underwater when all this happened, emerged to the happy prattle of the reunion, and looked less thrilled. He probably feared for his employment. He stepped from the pool and approached the threesome.

"Hi, Camille," he said.

"Boa. Where are they?"

Boa gestured to the guest house, and I got the impression they were talking about Odelia and Chase.

"Find them," Camille ordered, "and bring them to me."

She sounded like a warlord, ordering slaves to be fetched for execution.

Boa nodded curtly and stalked over to the guesthouse. Meanwhile, Dion and Damien had also joined the happy reunion, and even Kane had come running. The bulldog was yapping up a storm, barking at Camille as if he'd never seen her before, jumping up against Dion and Damien's legs, barking at Shayonne and Shalonda and generally creating a big fuss.

"That dog is such an idiot," Dooley said.

"He is," I agreed. Staring at the dog, a thought occurred to me, but when I tried to catch it, it vanished. There was something about Kane. But what?

Oh, well. It probably wasn't important.

Chapter 21

Laurelle Merritt's room wasn't much bigger than Eamonn's. The door was open so Odelia and Chase announced their presence by giving the doorpost a quick rap. Laurelle was sitting cross-legged on the bed, pictures and fashion magazines spread out all around her. She had a narrow, pale face, framed by a black bob, and was dressed in khaki shorts and a sleeveless maroon shirt.

"Hampton Cove police," Chase said. "Mind if we ask you a few questions, Miss Merritt?"

"Oh, of course," she said. "Um, come in. I'm sorry about the mess."

Odelia glanced around. The room was barely big enough to contain the bed, a vanity and a desk, and every available surface was crammed with stuff. Clothes, samples, magazines, makeup, wigs, clothes... Everything stuffed into the small space. "If you like we could do the interview outside," she said.

"Oh, no, that's fine. It probably won't take long, right?"

"No, just a few routine questions," Chase said. He was a lot kinder to Laurelle than he'd been to Boa or the others. Her story had touched a chord. "First off, where were you the night Shana Kenspeckle was killed?" he asked as he cleared away a few magazines and took a seat at the foot of the bed.

"I was right here. Asleep."

Odelia leaned against the desk. "Can anyone vouch for that?"

Laurelle shook her head. "I sleep alone, if that's what you mean. I don't have a boyfriend at the moment, so..." Her voice trailed off, and Odelia felt genuinely sorry for the young woman. She looked like a scared little mouse.

"We have to ask," she said softly.

"Of course. No, I get it. Just ask me anything you want."

This was probably a waste of time. It was obvious Laurelle wasn't the killer. She could probably hardly lift that cleaver, let alone wield it with such deadly force and precision. Still, they had to interview everyone on their list.

"There is one other thing we need to discuss, Miss Merritt," Chase said.

"Yes?" she asked, eyes large.

"We've been told about the tape."

"Yes?"

"The sex tape?" Odelia asked.

Shock appeared in the girl's eyes. "Who-who told you?"

"That's not important. Is it true?" asked Chase.

Laurelle buried her face in her hands. "Oh, no."

"I'm sorry to have to bring this up," said Chase. "But we need to know."

She nodded, then said, in a choked voice, "I made that tape back when I was still seeing this guy. He worked as a caterer and I thought he was the one." She shook her head. "So stupid. He convinced me that to make it in this business I should make a sex tape. It would put my name on the map. Give me exposure. I-I wasn't totally convinced but-but he was adamant."

Chase's jaw was working. If this caterer were here right now he'd probably give him a piece of his mind. And his fist.

Laurelle looked up. "So we made the tape and I sent it to

Shana, figuring she'd know what to do with it. She's got all these contacts, so... And she did show it around. To her sisters and all of their friends. To make fun of me. And to give me points for technique. Apparently I was so bad I was funny."

There was a note of bitterness in her voice, and Odelia didn't blame her. If something like this happened to her she'd probably die of mortification.

"Did they spread the tape beyond their circle?" Chase asked.

"No, thank God they didn't. Shana said the best thing would be to destroy the tape, as it could only ruin my reputation. So I did."

"Why didn't you quit your job?" Odelia asked. "After what Shana did to you it must have been hard to keep working for the Kenspeckles."

"It was at first, but this is basically my dream job. A lot of stylists would kill for this job. So I decided to suck it up." She produced a feeble smile. "It wasn't so bad. Shana apologized. Said she was totally out of line."

Chase asked some more questions, and so did Odelia, but it was pretty clear that this was not their killer, nor could she shed any light on the murder.

"All right, Miss Merritt," said Chase. "Thank you for your time. If there's anything else you can think of, give me a call." He handed her his card.

They left the room and walked back to the main house.

"We're nowhere," Chase said. "Absolutely nowhere."

"Did you check Shana's ex-boyfriend? Robin Masters?"

"Yeah, he's got an alibi. He's in Alaska. Writing his autobiography."

"Isn't he a little young to write his autobiography?"

But Chase didn't respond. Boa had joined them. He jerked his thumb in the direction of a woman in a fur coat who stood with her back to them.

"Lady wants a word with you, Detectives," Boa grunted.

"I think our luck just ran out, Poole," Chase said.

The woman turned, and Odelia recognized her. Camille Kenspeckle, the matriarch of the Kenspeckle clan. The woman she'd seen so many times on TV and the cover of countless magazines. And she did not look happy.

The moment Camille caught sight of them, she took off her sunglasses. There was a glint of steel in those eyes. "Detective Kingsley, I presume?"

"You presume right, Mrs. Kenspeckle."

"I'm calling off your investigation, Detective."

"You can't call off a police investigation, ma'am. It's not a photo shoot."

"I'm bringing in the FBI. This should have been treated as a terrorist attack from the beginning. You failed my little girl, Detective. You failed my family. But no more. I'm taking over, as I should have done from day one."

"This was not a terrorist attack," Chase insisted. "This was a homicide, and if you pull us off the investigation now we may never find the one responsible."

"You're through, Detective, and so are you, whoever you are," she said as she gave Odelia a supercilious glance. "This investigation is terminated."

Camille had a lot more things to say, and so did Chase, but Odelia decided she'd heard enough. It was clear they'd overstayed their welcome. While Chase argued with Camille, she went in search of her cats. She found them on top of the leather couch in the living room, chatting and chillaxing.

"What's going on?" Max asked.

"They're kicking us out," she said.

"See? I told you," said Max. "I told you this was the end."

"But they can't do that," Dooley said. "We're the cops."

"Camille has her own ideas about her daughter's murder," Odelia said. She picked up both cats and carried them off. "She's convinced it was a terrorist attack and that the FBI should take over."

"She's calling in the FBI?" Max asked.

"Yep. She said we've wasted enough time. She's taking her family back to LA, where she can protect them from the terrorists. She's going to trust the FBI to handle the investigation from now on and not us local yokels."

Max and Dooley followed her to the pickup. Five minutes later, Chase came walking up, his face a thundercloud. They all got into the car, and as they were pulling away from the house, down the long drive and out of the gate, a fleet of black Escalades came roaring up the drive and passed them.

"The Feds," Chase said. "Camille doesn't waste any time."

"So we're officially through?"

"Yes, we are," Chase said, his hands tight on the steering wheel.

"Can they do that? Just... swoop in and take over?"

"Afraid so." He glanced over. "It's out of our hands now, Poole."

"Pity we didn't catch the killer," Dooley said.

"Pity indeed."

"What's that?" Chase asked.

"Pity we didn't catch the killer."

"Yeah, damn shame."

"Uncle Alec won't like this."

"He doesn't have to like it. This time tomorrow the Kenspeckles will be gone, I'm pretty sure never to return. So it's none of our business anymore."

She settled back in her seat. Yep. This was the end, all right. The. End.

Chapter 22

"This is a nightmare," said Uncle Alec, worrying the few remaining strands of wispy gray hair on his head until they stood on end.

Odelia and Chase were ensconced in the Chief's office, discussing the unexpected turn their investigation had taken. A turn down the tubes.

"I talked to the FBI agent in charge. He told me to hand over any evidence we've managed to collect and they'll take it from here."

"Is he going to allow the Kenspeckles to fly out of here?" asked Odelia.

"Looks like. Camille wants her family safe and sound in that gated community where they all live. She's hired the best muscle in LA to protect them from the terrorists she thinks are gunning for them. Ex-special forces."

"I tried to explain we're not dealing with terrorists here," Chase said. "But Camille shot me down. She's convinced her family is under attack."

"I don't understand," Odelia said. "Why isn't the FBI on the same page? They can't possibly believe this was the work of some terrorist cell?"

"They're convinced the killer somehow managed to outsmart Boa's security team, and snuck in and killed Shana. It doesn't help that I can't offer them a suspect at this point. And arresting and being forced to release Dion Dread didn't exactly boost my credibility. Plus it infuriated the family."

"So what about the chloroform?" asked Odelia.

"What about it?"

"Don't terrorists usually plant a big bomb and blow up the whole place? Why sneak in, drug the entire household and target only one person? That doesn't sound like the work of a terrorist."

"Try telling them that. I'm done explaining to the Feds how to do their job."

"Did you tell them the note was an obvious fake?" asked Chase.

The Chief raised his hands and dropped them on the desk. "I'm the local moron here, guys. I'm a joke to these people. They don't listen to me."

"With the Kenspeckles gone so is our chance of finding the killer," Odelia said. Uncle Alec was right. This was a nightmare scenario, and the worst part was that they were exactly nowhere in their investigation. They'd talked to all the principals and so far she didn't have a single clue to the killer's identity.

"I don't know," said Chase. "You'd almost think Camille doesn't want her daughter's killer found."

"I'm sure she does," said the Chief, "but she doesn't trust you or me."

"When are they leaving?" Odelia asked.

"As soon as they're ready. They're packing up as we speak. The Feds will move them out in a motorcade, put them on a private jet and ship them off."

"I wonder if they're going to film this whole charade," said Odelia.

"Of course they will," said Chase. "This is all going to be on the show."

"Yeah, this will probably be the number one show of the season."

Odelia wondered why Max and Dooley hadn't discovered anything. Usually they were great at ferreting out those small details no one else was capable of discovering. Trivial things that could lead to a break in the case.

Her phone buzzed and she excused herself, stepping into the corridor. It was her mother. "Hey, Mom. Everything all right?"

"Did you know that you and Chase were on TV just now?"

"We were?"

"There's an item on the Kenspeckles, and they showed you and Chase leaving the house where they're staying. You were waving at the camera."

She remembered passing the camera crews camping out at the gate. "Yay. I'm famous."

"Yay."

"So what did they say?"

"Oh, nothing special. There was a lot of speculation about those black cars. They think it's either the Men in Black arriving or the FBI. Your grandmother thinks it's the Men in Black. I'm going with the FBI."

"What would the Men in Black want with the Kenspeckles?"

"Well, the newscaster is convinced the Kenspeckles are aliens, colluding with other aliens on their mother ship to colonize the planet. The other theory is that it's the FBI, and the local police are being sidelined. So what is it?"

"It's the FBI," she confirmed. "We're out. They're in."

"They're all aliens!" suddenly Gran's voice sounded over the phone. "One look at Camille is enough to know she's preparing an alien invasion. It's in the eyes, honey. No amount of plastic surgery can hide those alien eyes."

"The Kenspeckles are no aliens, Gran."

"Rubbish. The alien wears Prada. Don't be fooled by the fancy clothes."

"Will you give me back that phone?" Mom said. "What did you say?"

"The FBI has taken over, Mom. Our investigation is officially a bust."

"Oh, that's too bad. Can you invite your uncle and Chase over for dinner? We have barbecue. Does Chase like his mashed potatoes with garlic?"

She did a mental head thunk. Was this a time to think about barbecue? "I don't know, Mom. I don't know how Chase likes his mashed potatoes."

"Well, ask him, will you? This is important."

Of course it was. "I'll ask him."

"Oh, and I'm thinking about getting a dog."

"A dog? Why a dog? Don't we have enough cats?"

"Yeah, but dogs are affectionate. I hardly ever see Dooley or Harriet. They're either over at your place or out and about. Dogs stick to you like glue. I was thinking of getting myself a French Bulldog, like the one Shana Kenspeckle had? I saw him on TV—they did a rerun of some older episodes of the Kenspeckles—and he looks so cute!"

"Yeah, dogs love their owners," Odelia admitted. "Though Kane isn't as cute in real life as he is on TV, Mom. He's an annoying little yapper."

"Kane? Who's Kane?"

"Shana Kenspeckle's dog? The dog that's on the show?"

"Oh, but that's not Shana's dog, honey. Shana's dog was called Lil' Pim. He died last year, remember? Been with her since she was a kid. Kane used to belong to someone in Shana's entourage. They gifted Kane to Shana as a present when Lil' Pim died. To soften the blow."

Something went clickety click inside Odelia's head, like pieces of a puzzle falling into place. A sudden surge of excitement shot through her. "Do you remember who that dog belonged to, Mom?"

"Sure, um..." Her mother's voice trailed off. "Lemme think for a second. It'll come to me." There was some shuffling, then her mother's voice called out, "Mom! Who gave Shana Kenspeckle her new dog? I'm asking your grandmother, honey," she added, as if that wasn't obvious already.

"Damien LeWood!" Gran yelled back.

"Not her husband, her dog! Who gave her the dog?!"

There was some muffled discussion on the other end, and then Gran took over the phone again. "Is Chase coming over for dinner, honey? We're having barbecue."

She gritted her teeth. "Gran, who gave Shana her new dog?"

"Ask him if he likes his mashed potatoes with garlic. I think he does, but your mother has gotten it into her head he doesn't. Can you settle the argument? I'm right, aren't I? I'm always right. I've got a mind like a steel trap."

She heaved a deep sigh. "I'm sure Chase likes garlic."

"See! I told you so! He looks like a garlic-loving guy to me."

She tried to resist the urge to drag her grandmother through the phone. "Gran? The name?"

"Um... Lemme think for a minute. It's on the tip of my tongue."

Finally, her mother came on the line. "I just remembered, honey."

When her mother gave her the name, Odelia's jaw went slack.

It was the very last person she would have suspected.

Chapter 23

While Odelia and Chase were meeting with Chief Alec, Dooley and I went in search of Brutus and Harriet. It was time for an emergency meeting. I had once sworn a sacred oath that I would stand by my human, and I wasn't going to forsake her now. It was obvious this murder investigation meant a lot to Odelia, and so far we'd let her down.

"Do you really want to interrupt them on their hot date?" Dooley asked.

"Yes, I do. Catching the Kenspeckle killer is more important than a date."

"Not to Harriet and Brutus. They love dating. Dating is all they do."

"I don't care. We need to catch that killer. Dating can wait."

"Oh, fine," he said, though he didn't look happy. The prospect of catching Harriet and Brutus in the act under a park bench didn't appeal to him.

We trotted over to the park where only that morning I'd been stuck in a tree. It looked completely different during the day. Mothers were pushing baby strollers, tourists were licking ice creams, kids were kicking cans, teenagers were canoodling and senior citizens were reading the newspaper.

Most tourists were at the beach right now, soaking up the rays, but not all. Some enjoyed the peace and quiet of the park. And the shade. The north side of the park sloped down, and morphed into a stretch of sandy dunes, leading straight down to the beach. The park provided a welcome counterpoint of coolness. We passed the playground, with several toddlers playing in the sandbox, parents seated to the side to keep an eye on them.

"They could be anywhere," Dooley said. "This place is huge."

"Not that huge. And I'll bet they've chosen a quiet spot for their date."

"So they can have some privacy. Which we should probably give them."

"Do you or don't you want to find the killer?"

"Of course I want to find the killer. But I don't see how Brutus or Harriet are going to help us find him. If we can't solve this case, and Odelia and Chase and Uncle Alec can't solve this case, what makes you think they can?"

"It's the combined intelligence of the four of us that does the trick," I told him. "It's the power of the mastermind, Dooley. Four great minds provide a wisdom that is greater than its collective parts."

He stared at me dumbly, and I was starting to have second thoughts about this mastermind thing. I'd seen it on the History Channel once. How big tycoons rely on the convergence of great minds to come up with great ideas. I wondered if it also worked if some of those minds weren't as bright as others.

We headed to a denser part of the park, where Brutus and I had climbed that tree that morning. When I spotted a black tabby and a white Persian getting cozy under a bench, I knew we'd found them. "There they are."

"You talk to them," Dooley said, shaking his head. "I'm not doing this."

"Hey, guys," I said as I walked up to them, Dooley dragging his paws.

Brutus gave me his best glare. "What are you doing here?"

I told him in a few quick words what had transpired at the Kenspeckle place. It didn't help. "That still doesn't explain what you're doing here."

"Don't you see?" Harriet said. "Max wants our help to solve the case."

"You want my help?" asked Brutus, and he seemed genuinely surprised. "I thought you didn't need my help. Not after what happened yesterday."

"Well, it turns out I do need your help, Brutus," I said reluctantly.

A grin spread across his features. "You're admitting you can't do this without me?"

"That's... pretty much what I just said, yes."

The grin spread. "Just humor me, Max, and repeat that, will you?"

I rolled my eyes. Oh, God. He was back to his old obnoxious self. "Brutus, I need your help solving this case. I can't seem to do it without you."

"Like music to my ears. Tell me again, only this time act like you mean it."

Now it was my turn to glare at him. "Are you going to help or not?"

"You know what? I'll think about it. Let me get back to you."

"Oh, sugar plum. Don't be mean to Maxie. He's your friend now."

Brutus gave me a slap on the back. "Just messing with you, Maxie, baby. We're tree top buddies. We climbed a tree and survived. We're buds now!"

"Oh, you guys," said Harriet excitedly. "We're a team! It's what I've always wanted! We're best friends! The fearless foursome to the rescue!"

"Whoopee," Dooley muttered.

I didn't know what was worse: being Brutus's enemy or his buddy. We might have bonded to a certain extent up there in that tree, but that didn't mean we were bosom buddies now. Spend some time staring death in the face with another cat, and you'll start to feel a strange connection. It's not friendship, exactly. It's... complicated. Probably something only a shrink would understand. Still, I needed his help. We needed to figure this out.

"All right," I admitted. "We're all friends now. Happy?"

Harriet made funny little sounds, and she looked so excited she was about to spontaneously self-combust. She pressed her paws together. "Very happy."

"So what do you want us to do?" asked Brutus. "And make it snappy, cause Harriet and I have those dinner reservations at The Hungry Pipe."

"Dinner is hours away," said Dooley. "And it's not a reservation if you're going to eat leftovers on the roof of some dumb old restaurant."

"Hey, I'll have you know The Hungry Pipe is the place to be right now. And it is a reservation if your buddy can get you the best veal in town."

"All right, all right," I said, holding up my paws. "Let's not get into all that. We have a murder to solve, you guys, so we better get cracking."

"I think the dog did it," Harriet said decidedly.

"Kane? How do you figure that? Dogs don't swing meat cleavers with deadly force, or take out people with chloroform."

"No, but that dog was awfully quiet when the killer was doing his business. So the way I see it is that at the very least he's an accomplice."

"She's right," said Brutus. "That dog knows something. I mean, he's been barking up a storm, snapping at the heels of anyone in sight. So why wasn't he barking when someone killed his human? That doesn't make sense."

"You're right," I said, and suddenly that little tidbit of information dropped down from my memory banks and into the right slot. My face lit up with the light of intelligence, or at least I think it did. "Brutus! Harriet! You're brilliant! You just solved this case!"

"Huh?" asked Brutus.

"What?" asked Harriet.

"What are you talking about, Max?" asked Dooley.

"I know who did it! Kane told us!"

"He did? I don't remember," said Dooley.

"Neither did I. It was just one of those offhand comments. I didn't even pay attention to it at the time. But now I see he gave us the killer." I slapped Brutus and Harriet on the backs. "You solved the murder, you guys!"

Brutus puffed up his chest. "Of course I did." He paused. "So who is it?"

Chapter 24

Odelia and Chase stood outside the police station, watching as the motorcade slowly passed along Main Street. It stopped in the middle of the street. After a moment's delay, five Escalades parked on the side of the road.

"I wonder what's going on," said Odelia.

"Looks like they've decided to put in a little shopping," said Chase.

Odelia looked back when her uncle came out of the station.

"And? Any luck?" she asked.

"Nope. I talked to the guy in charge. I told him everything you told me, but he insists it's all circumstantial evidence. It didn't change his mind."

"Too bad we didn't know sooner," said Chase. "Where did this sudden brainwave of yours come from, anyway, Poole?"

She shrugged. "Just a hunch."

He eyed her curiously. "You've got some great hunches, Poole."

"That's Odelia for you," said the Chief. "She's always had an uncanny intuition when it comes to crime solving. Remember that time you figured out where Sonny Start had buried the body of his neighbor's Rottweiler? Everybody said the dog had run off, but you knew Sonny had poisoned him."

She shared a look of understanding with her uncle. He knew her cats had found the Rottweiler, not her. She watched now as Max and Dooley came trotting up. They looked excited. "We know who the killer is!" Max cried.

She crouched down. "So? Who is it? Don't keep me in suspense."

"Kane told us that first day. Only I completely forgot."

"Well, I think I know who the killer is, too. So let's hear it." When he gave her the name, she nodded. "Yep, that's what I thought."

He looked surprised. "How did you find out?"

"Thanks to you guys. You told me Kane didn't bark when the killer struck. And then my mother told me who gave Kane to Shana."

She rose, and saw that Chase was eyeing her wearily. "Talking to your cats again, Poole?"

"They like it when I talk cat."

"You sound so funny when you do that. You make these little cat sounds. Makes you sound almost like a real cat. It's the damnedest thing."

"Yeah, the damnedest thing," her uncle said, giving her a warning look.

Across the street, three burly FBI agents had stepped out of the first car, and checked around for a moment, probably looking for snipers targeting the Kenspeckles. Her mother was right. They really did look like the Men in Black. After a moment, they sounded the all-clear, and Camille Kenspeckle emerged from the vehicle. She was still dressed in her fur coat, Céline sunglasses on her nose, strappy black heels on her feet. She looked like a hundred thousand bucks, which was probably what she'd spent on her outfit.

Odelia watched as two FBI agents walked up to Darling's Dress Code, one of the more popular high-end clothing boutiques in town. The agents held the door for Camille, who strutted past them and disappeared inside.

"See? I told you they were putting in a little shopping," said Chase.

A surge of excitement raced through her. "This is our window. We have to confront her now, before it's too late." And before she could change her mind, she was already darting across the street in the direction of the store.

"Wait a minute!" Chase hollered, but she wasn't going to wait until the Kenspeckles boarded their private plane and got away. The FBI was right. They had nothing but circumstantial evidence. They needed a confession.

She walked up to the store and was about to go in when the two agents stopped her. "Sorry, ma'am. Store is closed. Private client tour in progress."

Of course. Camille wanted the store all to herself. She glanced in through the window, and saw that the Kenspeckle matriarch was browsing, a salesgirl in her wake. One more FBI agent had gone in, babysitting the reality star. She watched as Burr Newberry took a shot of the exterior of the shop and the FBI agents, who stood shaking their heads, and then also headed inside.

When this show aired, all of Hollywood would want a couple of Feds to go shopping with them. It would be the next big thing, up there with the dab.

She decided that the only way to confront Camille was to catch her off guard. She slipped into the alley two stores over, and made her way along the narrow street. Darling's had a back entrance, from the days it was still a liquor store. Locals boozers used to hang out back there, waiting for Kinnard Daym, who ran the store back in the day, to supply them with their favorite hard liquor in brown paper bags, blithely ignoring their wives' vetoes.

She tried the metal door, and found it neither guarded by Feds nor locked. She entered the store, and saw she was in a small storeroom. This was where Marina, Darling's Dress Code's current owner, kept her stock.

She opened the door connecting to the store, passed through a corridor which held the staff lavatory, and reached a painted chipboard door. She heard voices. One of them was Camille's. She pushed the door open and peeked in. No FBI and no bodyguards. Great. She stepped inside.

Marina was the first one to react. She was a stern-faced middle-aged woman with platinum hair and an unnaturally smooth brow. She'd actually gone to school with Odelia's mother, though Marina looked a decade younger. Her blue eyes cut to Odelia. "I'm sorry, honey. We're closed for business right now." She gestured to Camille, who stood holding a backless black gown in front of a full-length mirror, and whispered, "Private client viewing."

"Actually it's your client I'd like a word with."

Camille spotted her. Her face clouded. "You again. What do you want?"

"I need a word in private, Camille. It's about your daughter's murder."

Camille rolled her eyes. "Not again with the baseless accusations. I told you already. My family is the target of a terrorist plot. The FBI is handling things." She pointed an accusing finger at Odelia. "You tried to catch the killer and you failed. So you're done, missy. You're through."

"Just give me five minutes, and I'll tell you who killed Shana."

Camille stared at her, debating whether to call in the troops, or to give Odelia her five minutes. In the end, she said, "Start talking. And you," she added, pointing at Marina. "Get out. I'll call you when I need you."

"Yes, Mrs. Kenspeckle," Marina muttered, and hurried out.

"Shana wasn't murdered by a terrorist," Odelia said the moment they were alone. In a few words, she told Camille who the killer was, and why.

Camille looked at her thoughtfully. "And you know this how, exactly?"

"An anonymous witness came forward. She saw everything." It probably wasn't a good idea to mention this witness was in fact Clarice.

"You have a witness? Why didn't you say so before? This changes everything."

"The problem is that... the witness isn't available to testify."

She nodded. "A stalker, huh? Afraid to be prosecuted. Well, I'm certainly willing to make a deal. I won't come after her if she's willing to testify."

"She's not a stalker. She's... let's just say her testimony isn't admissible."

Camille threw up her hands. "So now what? We know who did it but we can't prove it."

"That's where you come in. We need to force a confession."

She explained her plan, hoping Camille would go along with it. To her surprise, the reality star didn't hesitate one moment. She gave Odelia a hug. "You found my daughter's killer, Miss Poole. How can I ever repay you?"

"Let's first get that confession," she said, awkwardly returning the hug. "And you don't have to repay me. My reward is seeing justice done."

Camille placed her phone to her ear, and made the call.

Laurelle walked in, looking anxious. “You wanted to see me, Camille?”

Camille gave her one of her rare smiles. “I wanted to talk to you alone, Laurelle. Away from the cameras and the police. Just the two of us. And this seemed like the only place I could do that. There’s been a break in the case.”

“A break? What do you mean?”

“I just got a call from one of the police officers working on the case. A witness has come forward, Laurelle. A witness who saw Shana’s murder.”

Laurelle’s already pale face became even paler. “A-a witness?”

“An eyewitness who... saw you in Shana’s room that night.”

The stylist’s eyes went wide. “But that’s impossible. I wasn’t anywhere near Shana’s room that night. I told the police already. I was in bed.”

“Someone was watching, Laurelle,” said Camille. “Someone was watching through the window. They saw you murder my daughter.”

“That’s just crazy! How can this witness have seen me? The killer wore a mask. Whoever this is, they’re lying, Camille. I would never kill Shana!”

“That’s what I first thought. The thing is, the dog didn’t bark, Laurelle.”

Laurelle looked at Camille as if she was crazy. “The dog didn’t bark?”

“That’s right. You know Kane. That stupid mutt barks at everything and everyone. But that night he didn’t bark when the killer attacked Shana.”

“So? That doesn’t prove anything.”

“It proves everything. You gave that dog to Shana. You’re the only one he never barks at, because you’re his owner and he knows that.”

"The killer could have drugged Kane, like he drugged everyone else."

Camille shook her head decidedly. "I believe you killed Shana, Laurelle."

"But, Camille—"

"The police also told me you used to work at your uncle's butcher shop until you left your hometown to become a stylist in LA. They told me you were very handy with the meat cleaver. In fact your uncle told them you were an ace. That for a girl of your size and build you packed quite a punch."

"I... I don't know what to say. This is just... ridiculous."

Camille fixed her with an implacable look. "Why did you do it? Was it because of that silly sex tape? Yes, Shana told me all about that. How that tape was your claim to fame. She even sent me a copy of the silly thing."

Laurelle's lips tightened and she went still. "You saw my tape?"

"Of course I saw your tape. Everybody did. We all had a good laugh. The thing was hilarious. Did you really think it would make you famous?"

"That tape wasn't Shana's to distribute. I gave it to her in confidence."

"It's a sex tape, Laurelle. If you didn't want people to see it, why did you make it in the first place?"

Laurelle shook her head. She'd moved back, and twin dots of crimson had appeared on her cheeks. Out of nowhere, a knife suddenly manifested in her hand. "You're just as bad as your asshole daughter, Camille. I should have taken care of you and your family a long time ago."

Camille eyed the knife nervously. "What are you doing?"

Laurelle's lips curled up into a cruel smile. "What do you

think I'm doing? I'm going to put my carving skills to good use. This time without a witness."

"You won't get away with this. Everyone will know it was you."

The stylist shrugged. "I'll just cut myself. Tell the cops the terrorist struck again and I barely escaped with my life. I'll even throw in a full description this time. Only for you, help will come too late, of course. You'll be dead."

"Why did you do it, Laurelle? Why did you kill my daughter?"

"For the same reason I'm going to kill you. Because you deserve it," she spat. "You think you're so high and mighty. Sitting on your throne of money and fame and power. You think you can mock and ridicule everyone else. Well, no more. I deserve a spot in the limelight, just like you, and I'm going to get it. That tape was supposed to put me out there, but your daughter sabotaged everything. She didn't want the competition. She could have made me part of her inner circle but instead she chose to keep me down."

"You're crazy," said Camille. "No silly sex tape could have made you famous. It would simply have made you the laughing stock of the world."

Laurelle stuck out her chin. "You know it's all about celebrity endorsement. If Shana had endorsed my tape, it would have put my name on the map."

"You're deluded, honey. It doesn't work that way. Shana was famous not because of some elusive celebrity endorsement but because she had talent and worked her ass off to make it in this business. Success doesn't fall from the sky. Shana had to work hard to make a success of herself, and she wasn't going to hand it to you on a silver platter just because you felt entitled."

"You're so wrong. I'm not entitled. I'm talented. I just needed a break."

"Drop that knife. It's over. You killed Shana and you're going to jail."

"It isn't over until I say it is. You and your family are going to suffer. I'm going to kill every last one of you. First I'll carve you up like a brisket, and then I'm going to do the same to your rotten kids. I won't rest until all the Kenspeckles are nothing but a bunch of cadavers rotting in the ground."

"You're insane," said Camille, throwing up her hands. "Why didn't I see this before? When this is over I'm going to have a word with your employment agency. This is just ridiculous."

"One more thing before I slice you to ribbons," said Laurelle. "Give me the name of the witness."

"I told you, it was Kane," said Camille.

"I should never have given my precious baby to Shana," said Laurelle. "I knew she wouldn't appreciate it. I just felt sorry for her after Lil' Pim died."

"Well, Kane was the witness."

"Quit messing around, Camille," said Laurelle, gesturing with the knife. "Tell me the name of the witness."

Odelia stepped from behind the curtain. "That would be me."

Laurelle's eyes widened in shock. "You! What are you doing here?!"

"Telling Camille what's going on."

"*You* saw me that night?"

"A family friend did."

Laurelle took a step toward her. "Give me the name or I'll gut you right now. One slice is all it takes to spread your guts all over the floor so you can watch yourself bleed to death."

"Sounds like fun," Odelia said. "But I think I'll pass." She shook her head. "And here I thought you were the victim. You sure fooled me."

"I am the victim. I'm the victim of Kenspeckle greed."

"You made that tape, didn't you?" asked Odelia. "That was your idea."

"Of course it was my idea. I devised the whole plan. You don't think I escaped that shit town of Armada, Illinois just to spend my life slaving away for the Kenspeckles, do you? I came to LA to become rich and famous, only this asshole here doesn't want to share. So now I'll make her pay. And I'll make you pay," she said, making a slashing gesture in Odelia's direction.

"I wouldn't do that if I were you," a voice sounded from the door. Chase had appeared, and he was accompanied by the FBI agent in charge.

Laurelle stared at them, completely taken aback. "I... the terrorist was here, and... he attacked me and..."

"I don't think so, Laurelle," said Burr as he stepped from behind the curtain. He had his camera mounted on his shoulder and pointed at Laurelle.

The knife dropped from her hand and fell to the floor. "You filmed me?"

"Yep. Got it all on tape." He tapped his camera proudly. "A real doozy."

It was over, and she knew it. Chase stepped forward, and outfitted the fallen stylist with a nice set of shiny new handcuffs. Laurelle looked at Odelia. "Who was the witness? Who saw me that night? I need to know."

Odelia shrugged. "There was no witness. I just made that up."

The girl's face contorted into an expression of rage. "I hate you. I hate all of you! And I hate you most of all, Camille Kenspeckle! I'll get you for this!"

"Join the line," said Camille with a satisfied smile. "Oh, God," she said as she turned to Odelia. "I can't thank you enough, honey. If not for you I'm pretty sure that monster would have murdered my entire family."

"That seems to have been her plan all along," said Odelia. "Only she wanted to take her time. Kill you one at a time and make you suffer as long as possible." She glanced at the camera, which was pretty much in her face now. "Um, could you stop filming now?"

Camille grinned. "Why? You're going to be next season's biggest star."

Two cats came darting in, and she picked them both up. "These are my stars," she said. "My biggest stars."

Pity she couldn't tell the world they were the ones who caught Laurelle. Then again, sometimes real heroes went uncelebrated.

"Mom," said Shayonne as she came darting in. "Is it true Laurelle is the killer?"

"Yes, it's true," said Camille.

"No way!" Shalonda cried, close on her sister's heel. "Did you get her confession on tape?"

"Yes, we did."

The two sisters exchanged high fives. "Best. Show. Ever!"

Odelia shook her head and walked out. Keeping up with the Kenspeckles was a tough proposition, but at least she hadn't sustained permanent damage.

Epilogue

Dusk was falling and Dooley and I were seated on the swing Doctor Tex had installed on the back porch. Gran was sitting next to us, patiently waiting for dinner to start. Tex was whipping beef ribs onto the barbecue, joining the burger patties and sausages already sizzling on the grill. Uncle Alec was helping him by swigging back a Corona and being generous with his advice.

My stomach grumbled as the delicious scent caressed my nostrils. We'd already been fed a few slivers of raw sausage, and now we were waiting for the barbecue feast to start, cooked up by the barbecue maestro himself.

Even though Tex warned against artery-clogging red meat on a daily basis to his patients, when he wasn't on duty he liked to treat himself to some choice artery-clogging beef ribs himself. He argued that if God didn't want us to have barbecue, he shouldn't have made it taste and smell so darn good.

Chase and Odelia were seated at the white plastic table Marge had placed in the garden. They were deeply engrossed in conversation, probably clearing up the last few details about the murder case. Marge was busy in the kitchen, doing something with potato salad, and putting the finishing touches on the chocolate cake she was baking. Brutus and Harriet were snuggling at Odelia's feet. They'd canceled their romantic evening for dinner with the fam.

Movement suddenly caught my eye, and when I glanced over I saw that Clarice was sneaking through Odelia's garden. She disappeared into the house. Odelia had decided that in celebration of the fact that Clarice had provided the telling clue to catch the killer, she would adopt her. Only Clarice wasn't in favor of being adopted. She preferred to roam wild and free. As a compromise, she had accepted that she could always get food and shelter at Odelia's if she wanted to. She now even had a big bowl with her name on it—literally. That was actually my idea. I didn't want Clarice stealing my food.

You might say us cats have a problem with sharing. You might be right.

I saw Clarice stalk out of the house again. Our eyes locked, and she gave me an almost imperceptible nod before skulking off, licking her whiskers.

I turned a lazy eye back to the garden, and I was struck by an outrageous sight. Chase was leaning into Odelia, and planting a kiss on her lips. And she wasn't even fighting him! Of course, after being forced to watch Shalonda and Boa in the pool, no display of carnal love had the power to shock me anymore. Still, this wasn't something I'd ever expected to see in my lifetime.

"Max?"

"Uh-huh."

"Odelia and Chase are kissing."

"I know, Dooley."

"I mean, they're actually kissing!"

"I know! I have eyes. I can see."

"Um. And it looks like it's a real kiss. Like, with tongue and all?"

"Yep, that's a real kiss all right," said Gran. She sighed wistfully. "Boy, that brings back a few memories." She looked happy. "I knew this was gonna happen. I just knew it. And not a minute too soon either."

"What do you mean?" I asked.

"If she's going to provide me with a brace of great-grandchildren she needs to get a move on. I can't wait around forever, you know."

"What do you mean you won't wait around forever?" asked Dooley.

"In case you hadn't noticed, I'm not getting any younger, boys, and neither are you. If we want to hear the pitter-patter of little feet, it's now or never."

Dooley and I stared at each other, aghast. Pitter patter of little feet? "You mean... babies?" Dooley cried, his voice rising an octave in sheer horror.

"What do you think I mean? The pitter patter of mice? Of course babies."

"But, but, but... I don't want babies!" Dooley squeaked.

"Yeah, if Odelia has babies, what's gonna happen to us?" I asked, a sense of panic settling in my stomach and even driving away my nice pre-barbecue buzz. I knew what happened when babies were born: it was in with the new, and out with the old. In this case, Dooley and Harriet and me.

"Nothing's gonna happen to you," Gran said with a chuckle. "As long as you promise to take good care of the young 'uns, you'll be just fine."

"This is it," Dooley said miserably. "This is the end."

"Yeah," I echoed. "We're doomed."

"No, you're not," said Gran. "You'll always be our babies. And if you keep catching killers like you do, you'll probably even get a medal or something."

"I don't want a medal," I said. "I just want to be Odelia's baby."

"Relax, boys. Nobody's going to replace you. On the contrary, babies are fun, and they smell great. And what's more, if Odelia and Chase get hitched, your little buddy is going to move in with you. Won't that be a barrel of fun?"

Dooley and I stared at Brutus, who gave us a pinkie wave, then at each other, and we burst into tears. Our lives had officially gone down the toilet.

About Nic

Nic Saint is the pen name for writing couple Nick and Nicole Saint. They've penned 50+ novels in the romance, cat sleuth, middle grade, suspense, comedy and cozy mystery genres. Nicole has a background in accounting and Nick in political science and before being struck by the writing bug the Saints worked odd jobs around the world (including massage therapist in Mexico, gardener in Italy, restaurant manager in India, and Berlitz teacher in Belgium).

When they're not writing they enjoy Christmas-themed Hallmark movies (whether it's Christmas or not), all manner of pastry, comic books, a daily dose of yoga (to limber up those limbs), and spoiling their big red tomcat Tommy.

Sign up for the no-spam newsletter and be the first to know when a new book comes out: nicsaint.com/newsletter.

Also by Nic Saint

The Mysteries of max

Purrfect Murder
Purrfectly Deadly
Purrfect Revenge

The Mysteries of Bell & Whitehouse

One Spoonful of Trouble
Two Scoops of Murder
Three Shots of Disaster
A Twist of Wraith
A Touch of Ghost
A Clash of Spooks
The Stuffing of Nightmares
A Breath of Dead Air
An Act of Hodd

Ghosts of London

Between a Ghost and a Spooky Place
Public Ghost Number One
Ghost Save the Queen

Witchy Fingers

Witchy Trouble
Witchy Hexations
Witchy Possesions
Witchy Riches

Other Books

When in Bruges
Once Upon a Spy
The Whiskered Spy
The Ghost Who Came in from the Cold
Enemy of the Tates

45014675R00119

Made in the USA
Middletown, DE
22 June 2017